I0748244

D E S K C L E R K

Kenny Mooney

__FLAT__FIELD__PRESS__

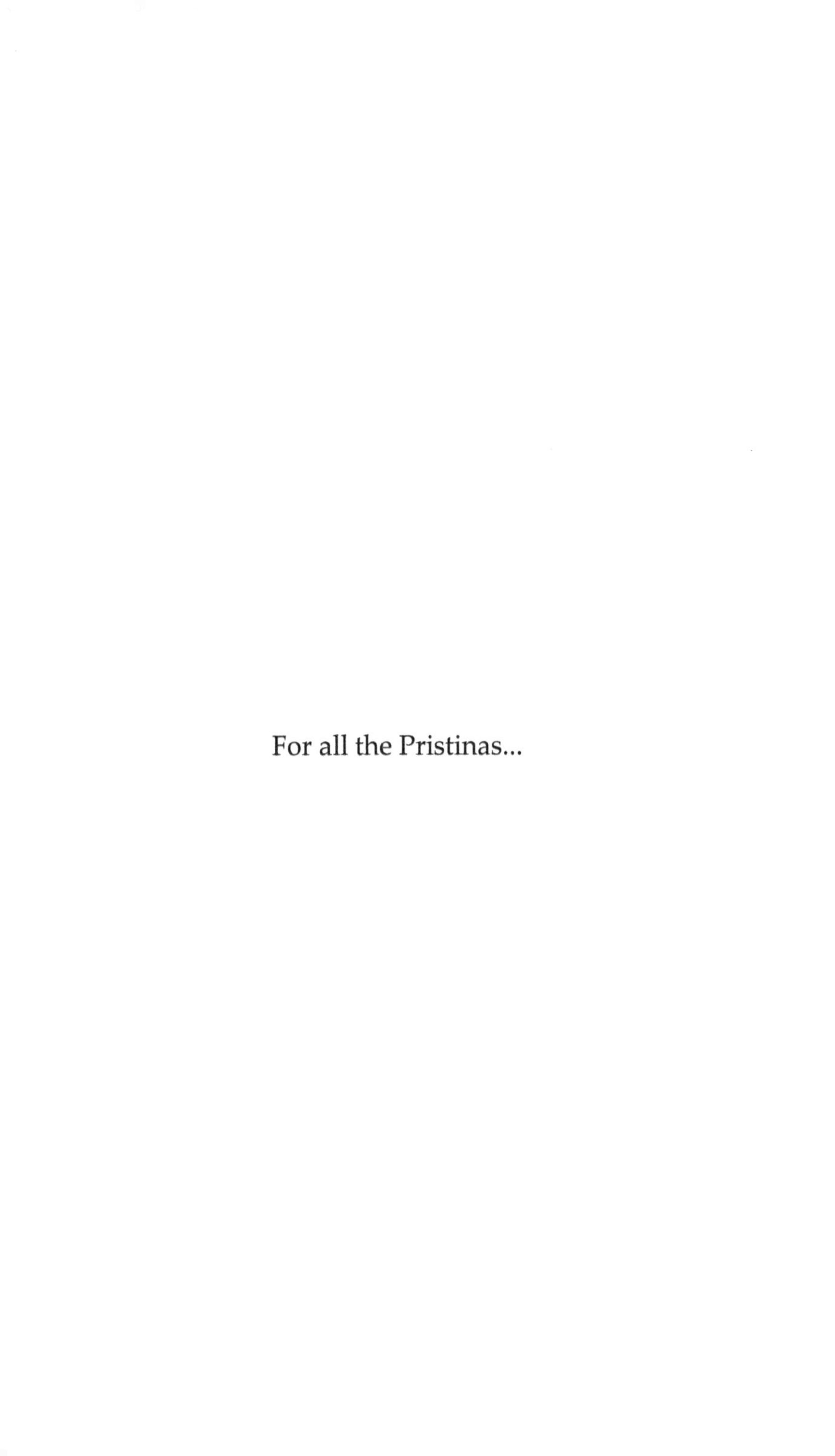

For all the Pristinas...

APARTMENT

She lies sleeping on the bed. The walls around her shimmer amber city light, bleeding in through ragged curtains, floods of sick yellow—a diseased pornography in vomit-orange. It makes us blink and hide. Under the covers and in our closets, we hide. We look for doors to close. In time.

She breathes deep and hard through cracked and dry lips. Red as her blood. Now black—now red—now dry as a barren field. Her body rolls like a vast ocean, and my touch dips just below her surface, barely reaching her dark, unknowable depths. She is wax—soft and cold, fingertips sink into her butter skin. She is coated in a sheen of photocopier toner. And in that fine, umbral dust I trace shapes, the contours of her body—the battlefield of the apartment. I walk these halls as I walk her halls, through her cavernous openings. Her mouth opens, teeth and tongue slick and dark. I leave sooty fingerprints on the sick yellow walls when I feel my way around her rooms. On her furniture my dirty hands fumble. When I look in the mirror I see a face smeared in black.

She is slowly suffocating under the strips of false daylight. With the sweet stink of monster machines—printers, faxes, photocopiers. With the heat and the airlessness. Her eyes are ringed in the shadows of sleepless nights spent staring into the darkness. Bloodshot bruises on the pristine paper-white of her skin. Her scent is no longer her own. She smells sugary and sick. She tastes of ink and nylon. Her veins run with the black blood of fax toner. She spits it on the mirrors in the bathrooms, smearing it across the glass in streaks, painting patterns that resemble the shape of her face. And in those patterns she sees repetition. She sees maps.

Pristina—the photocopy girl, they called her. The nickname clung to her like the office scent that filled her pores, her hair. Our mutually precarious existences had brought us together in the corporate hell of the city, and though we try, we are never able to wash away that stench. Each day she stands naked in the shower, weeping as the water pours black and blue from her body—all the ink running out of her. I hold her and carry her to the bedroom.

We lie together.

Through most of these nights she is silent. The sun rises, and in its blast we return again to the city. But some nights she talks for hours. Her dreams. Her nightmares. Sometimes she stutters like a broken machine and noises emerge from her mouth that are no language ever heard. Those times she seems to fall into a seizure, and I see her contort her body into awkward, impossible shapes and angles. She throws herself against walls, static surges from her lips and I plead with her to stop. Those are the longest of nights.

Her days are spent in the small office photocopier and print room, a cell of noise and machine, of paper and ink. These thousands of letters she prints, she copies, she mails into the world. She mutters the names as she stands there alone. She repeats them over and over, tracing fingers over the warm, damp lettering, smudging those words.

Sometimes she sees her own name on those address labels and letterheads. She sees them going into envelopes, sealed into mail bags. She tastes the ink from her fingers, feels the presence of others, her namesakes. Her copies.

She is replicated many times over. She knows it. She feels it. She is copied as she copies, as she prints, as she slaves to those machines. And through the clotted veins of the city her copies live and breathe. In those concrete corridors copies of copies of copies have jobs and careers and families that are not her own. They are men and women, different but all the same. She feels at times as though she is a copy herself, and on Monday mourning when the sense of loss is greatest, she looks at herself and feels as though she is beginning to flicker, to fade. She reminds herself that she is the original, but they all think that.

She tests me sometimes. What's my name? she asks, looking at me, lying beside her on the bed. I make up different ones each time, teasing her. She smiles thinly and laughs, then goes to look at herself in the bathroom mirror. I watch her push and pull at her face, staring into the reflection of her eyes for long moments. She checks her fingernails, black with the ink and dust of the office. For long minutes she stands there, staring. I tell her she doesn't look any different, that her face is the same as yesterday.

She ghosts her way through those copy lives, leaking into them like the ink she inhales each day, the ink in her blood. It's what powers her, a fluid that enables her transition from her body to theirs. I see her in the bed, lying naked in a pool of murky red-black. It oozes from her pores, her mouth, her nose. I touch her face, enamel-white like hospital gowns soaked in bleach, and I feel the cold of her body seep into me. Her skin smells so stained, tastes so toxic. She is a multitude of other lives. A polyglot of existence.

And in those other lives she becomes entangled, becomes obsessed. I wonder now whether she remembers who she is. Some days she seems so washed through, so vacant. When she walks through rooms the shadows that leap across walls don't appear to be hers, and when she speaks her voice has an unusual edge, the hiss of distortion, the low crunch of cracking concrete. The way she looks at me, with anger flaring, or with a dangerous lust, frightens me. Her personality slips and slides as her movements become precise and deliberate. She picks her way over the ink-stained furniture, colours flashing from monochrome to neon arcs. When she kisses me it is cold—poisonous water pours into my throat. I touch fingers to my wet lips and they come away slick and dark.

When she wakes up, she talks about the copy life she shared some time with, about the job, the family. Sometimes these are happy stories. Her smile glows and she laughs. Then there are the times that are not so happy. Some of her copies are sad. They are alone. They live with squalor and abuse. They are violence and nightmare. Those times Pristina wakes with bruises, black and blue and green, along her arms, her face. She talks very little about them. She just crawls to me and sobs.

It's the good episodes that are the worst. In those she gets a glimpse of the possible, of what her life could be like. Her longing, her desperation, it turns to melancholy. She starts to talk then of escaping, of running away from this. Leave it all, she says. I don't understand what she means, and tell her we don't have the money to just leave our lives. She turns away from me then, whispering to herself, a kind of coldness creeping into her.

Her copy selves degrade, grow less and less defined. She finds it harder to reach them, to slip into them. She has her favourites, the ones with happy lives, and she likes to revisit them, despite the depression that follows. My only escape, she says.

But in time they all fade. She says it feels itchy when she is ghosting with a copy who is badly eroded. Her vision is grainy and she feels as though she is coiled in wire. I watch her in these moments, twisting on the bed, her eyes flickering beneath her dark eyelids. Her skin grows red and angry, a rash spreading over her, irritated by the abrasive aura.

And then small muscle twitches. Her body begins to move like the surface of the sea. She heaves and rolls. Her mouth opens and a roar of surf emerges, becoming a scream. She thrashes—a violent spinning storm, a tangle of bedding and noise. I watch as she lives through the death of one of her copies. I watch while she feels the draining, the erosion of existence, the blurring away to the black. The nothing.

Now there is a rage that boils at the very centre of her, a rage that spits and hisses and tears down plaster walls, burning and seething, a star burning itself into oblivion. A star preparing to explode. She throws her anger into her copies, into her faded other lives. She throws hate and destruction into those photocopy people. Her army grows as her rage grows, and daily she copies herself, unleashing more and more, degrading herself as she multiplies.

Her obsession now. The growth of her many. The increasing numbers of copies out there in the city—the building of her army. What used to unite us, now divides us. Each day she returns to the city, to the office, to false daylight and machines. Each day she basks in the blast of neon and amber and yellow. I see her fade. I see her beginning to dissolve as ink in water. And I cannot stop her.

She looks at me with eyes dark and red, with the burning vision of someone ready to annihilate. Quivering angles cut shadows deep, her hands shaking as she touches my face and I flinch. Cool skin hot brow, she tastes my sweat with her tongue and it makes her smile. She tells me not to be afraid.

She spends her nights ghosting through those copy people, setting to work, putting plans in place. I can only wait at the bedside, hoping there will be no more horrific screaming. In the mornings she scans newspapers, sits with her face pressed close to the television screen, watching, waiting. An expectation is growing in her. Red circles in ink-print signal signs from her army. She covers the bedroom walls with stories, photographs, headlines. She shows me these triumphs, the victories of her forces. You see? she says, it begins now. Her hands move over those black pages, delicate, sensual. Ways she used to touch me.

I no longer sleep. I lie with Pristina, in a room wrapped in the newspaper ink of her spreading war. I watch the shades of her copies moving around the rooms, phasing in and out, flickering as old film images. At first these apparitions startled me, and I recoiled as they walked through walls and stopped to stare at me, huddled there next to their original version. Their eyes, those copy eyes, moved from me to her, and they stared at her for long hours and as dawn encroached on the city they melted away into the early morning orange, leaving small damp patches of tears.

They no longer concern me, and they no longer take notice of me. They come to watch her sleep, perhaps to watch over her, just as I watch over her. They stand in groups around the bed, kneeling beside her. Each night there are more of them. Pristina's army grows in numbers.

Sometimes I wake in pools of ink bleeding out of Pristina as she inhabits the lives of her various copies. Sometimes there are tears, damp kisses across the bedding and pillows— my face. Everything is stained a watercolour of blue-black. During the night her breath is a mist of fine printer ink, gasping out into the air of the room. It blooms and drifts, settles on furniture, sticks to the walls and ceiling. Each morning I wash that residue from my face, spit it into the sink. Each morning I try to become clean.

Now as the sun rises over the city and weak daylight shines through the blinds, I find myself alone in the bed. Pristina's side is cold. I call out her name, three syllables that crash like rolling waves.

The silence of the apartment urges me to rise. Standing from the bed my feet sink into soft, wet carpet. I look down and see water spreading out across the floor from the bathroom. I hear the lap, the gentle caress of it running from taps, of it pouring over the sides of the bathtub.

All quiet now. All still. As though the world has stopped spinning and the breath in my lungs has been hushed. All gone. All but that sound. It builds as I move to the door, a violent crescendo, an orchestra of rivers rushing towards a great cataract.

Water red. Like evening sky. Red like stabbing. Water red like. Pouring water red over floor, red over tiles, seeping. Water stained red. Atomic clouds bloom. Bleeding bloody water red.

Time sears through my veins. Pristina's wet, naked body sprawling across me, across the floor, water red and skin drained to grey-white, the colour of dead fish. We tangle in a sick dance, a terrible love-making there on the bathroom floor, desperation slipping. That moment in the film when the soundtrack drops out—only the gasps, the whimpers, the cries.

We shift to monochrome.

We shift to deep focus.

We shift.

Hospitals are places without definition. They sit between worlds—liminal spaces in white render. Scrubbed down with chemical cleansers, populated by shades in the shapes of people. Just uniforms. No air moves through those corridors. No colour pulses. The only light that bleeds within those stone veins is a blinding white. Hospitals make everything shadow. Everything becomes indistinct. All that is solid melts into the air. Becoming ghost.

Here the tortured. Here the insane, the sick, the diseased of mind. Here those twisted inside by plague, disfigured by injury.

Hear the suicides.

Hear the wailing. Hear the screaming. Hear Pristina raging at nurses, clawing blood from them as they move around her, white ghosts, pale blue figures. She shimmers violent orange. The air around her thrums in pulses.

See me standing motionless before this thrashing of curtains and bedding and limbs. Motionless and powerless. Pristina's words colour the air, and nurses gasp, mutter as they leave her bedside. Never been so treated. Never been so abused.

Hospital hum around us now. The blurring of voices, air conditioning, wheels on floors, footsteps, crying. Screaming.

I sit by her side and beg for an explanation. Hard plastic chair. Sterile floors. I grab her by the shoulders—shake her. What were you thinking?

But her body is stiff with fear. Her eyes dart around, from face to face as nurses and patients and staff move around the ward, the corridors of white descending. She grabs my hand and squeezes, so tight, her nails digging. She mutters about leaving, about eyes, about being trapped. I see no threats. I tell her there is no danger, that she is safe here.

And she glares at me with eyes that burn through. You can't keep me safe. Hissed through teeth. Hand snatched away.

She turns away now, wrapped in herself, in her white cotton sheets. Her back.

And I know that I am a failure in her eyes. That I have failed to do what I always promised — to protect her. Even from herself. All the horror, all the terrible things she saw, the things she had spent her life hiding from. The worst of all of them was herself. I should have seen it coming. I should have known from the moment her army began to grow. Instead I was an observer. A voyeur.

She turns back towards me. Crying now. And as she wipes her tears, she smears black ink across her face, forming a sinister mask.

I'm sorry, she says, her hand reaching out to me. I tell her I don't understand. She nods. I know, she says.

Returning to the apartment, to the scene of both our failures. The smell of damp carpet—the itch of blood. The bathroom floor streaked in red, and handprints on the walls from our desperation. I lift the carpet and try to soak up the water in the bathroom, towels and rags stuffed into corners. And bleach making my hands as red as the stained floor and walls. I try to clean it away. I try to become clean.

This apartment—a flat black field.

I visit her each day. They keep her in a room on her own. A room with no handle on the inside. This is to keep her from distressing the other patients, they tell me. This is to allow her wounds to heal—her physical and emotional wounds. I meet her psychiatrist in the corridor during one visit. A tall man, the ceiling against his back like an arc of sky. He talks through round spectacles and leaking blue pens. He talks of things I know nothing about in a voice that is running water. He talks of medication. And the smell of stale coffee. He talks of institutionalisation.

Pristina smiles and opens her arms to me. She likes the psychiatrist, she tells me, he is patient and friendly. They meet every morning for an hour and they just talk, about all kinds of things. About her hopes, her fears, her doubts. I want to ask about the army, about her copies, but I smile and nod and try to be the things I failed to be before. I try to be supportive and interested. Caring. Yet a weariness grows within me. A fatigue. Most days I lack the strength to face my own life, the world and all the people with their faces and mouths spilling words. Pristina has worn me thin. I am riddled with tiny tears, rips. Body slowly being pounded down to dust. She doesn't mean to. She can't help it. Pristina glows so hot and with such violence that she sears anything and anyone that gets too close. A star burning so terribly. And I have been in her orbit for so long now.

Then the mood changes in the room. Shadows grow long, darken. The air bristles with insect wings. She leans towards me, eyes darting left to right. There is someone else, she says, there is another. He lurks.

Her voice crackling, hissing with hush, she tells me that someone in the hospital is watching her. She feels his eyes all the time, but mostly at night. She sees shades, blurred shapes by the door, moving through the hall. Sometimes a sound—the clearing of a throat, a breath. And the smell. Of chemicals—surgery-clean scalpel smells. She shakes her head when I ask if she has reported this, and I wonder. I wonder what the medication is doing to her.

You believe me, she says with an uncertain smile. I hold her face in my hands, lost in her vulnerability, her concealed rage. Of course, I tell her, and she looks unconvinced. For a moment I'm sure I have hurt her, lost her attention for the day. Then she is talking about how nice the nursing staff have been, how tired she is, how cold the room feels.

Her moods often shift in this way, sudden changes in angle. One moment detached, staring at the sky beyond the window, the next clawing at me in a wild sexual frenzy, so aggressive I have to fight with her. And she laughs at me.

Some days she asks about her copy army and if they are looking after me. I tell her I haven't seen them since she went into hospital. She seems confused, biting her lip. Perhaps they are watching me? she says, and looks around the room. I follow her gaze, but we both see nothing.

To be let down by me is one thing, a failure that perhaps she expected all along. A human failure. Now Pristina begins to wonder if she has been abandoned by those fragments of her own self. Have they left me? she asks. I don't know, I tell her. I try to think of something reassuring to say. Maybe the medication has caused the delusion to pass. But didn't

I also see them? Didn't I too suffer the same delusion? Perhaps it was a kind of sickness and for a while I was infected as well. Now maybe I am cured.

I find a reason to leave the room for a few minutes. To get air. To get away. There is the smell of chemical cleansers in the hall, a harsh kind of clean, unnatural and metallic. I find myself swallowing hard, a scratching itch at the back of my throat, like grit only it won't clear.

I wander along corridors, the reflections of strip-lights in the floor and my twisted shape lurching. I pass other wards, other patients. They sit alone in rooms, or with family. The old, the frail, the infirm. Yellowed eyes, bleary with the years follow me, and I look away. I look only at my distorted reflection, all awkward angles and a blur of limbs. I wonder if that is how I am really moving, lumbering along, a confused mass of arms and legs.

A figure moves ahead of me, gliding from a ward into the corridor. A shape in white, hair dark and flowing. Pristina?

I try to call out to her but my throat is dry. My mouth full of gum. What is she doing out of bed? Why is she wandering around the hallways? I start after her, watching her moving through groups of doctors and nurses. Is she floating? She starts to blur, dissolving into water. The other people, the hall, everything else sharp focus, clear, but she is becoming a blind spot, too bright to look at. Painful.

Panic rising like vomit. My heart is pounding, breath ragged. I'm staggering, half-running through the corridor, chasing Pristina. I think of our conversation about her copy army, and wonder—

Now the faces of people are just a mess of colour. There is no shape to anything anymore. The hallway is twisting, corkscrewing before my eyes, the white of the walls is being sucked into the dark of some doorway ahead.

And I see her standing. I see her walking. I see her enter that doorway.

A sound of crashing metal and I spin. The light is so harsh. I blink away tears. There is a wheelchair close to me, lying on its side. A stunned porter is staring at me. His mouth moves. All I hear is rushing. Water surging. A body splashing in a bath.

I feel myself against the wall, pressed against the smooth surface, now like skin. I look back towards the doorway, ignoring the rising sound behind me that must be voices. Someone touches my shoulder and I push away from the wall, shrugging free of them. I move towards the dark.

An office. Inside I see a desk, papers and files piled high. A worn leather armchair. There is the smell of something rank in the air. Stale sweat. Coffee. This somehow seems familiar to me, though I have never been here before. Nausea rises up through me. Something is dripping from my nose. My lips and chin feel wet. I lean against the open doorway, cold sweat, shivering.

She isn't here.

Voices from the hall rush up from the slow depths of the ocean to shrieking clarity. I look around and someone is pointing at the floor.

Red blotches smeared by my footsteps, my blood-trail down the freshly bleached corridor. Now the ringing in my ears. Now the thundering. The draining away of vision into a swirl of jarred bones and darkness.

I awake to darkness. To the terror that someone has their hand over my eyes and mouth. I gasp—snatch at empty air. For a second I am drowning, throat and lungs full of water. It goes on and on, this second, stretching out for hours, as my arms flail around, snatching at air, clawing at emptiness.

Here, lying on a leather sofa, curtains drawn over a small window. Weak shafts of sunlight cut through here and there, and in the gloom I can just make out the shape of a desk, piled high with papers, books, files. A cabinet of medicines. Drugs. Surgical tools. The smell— clean and abrasive. And a shape behind the desk moves, sitting upright but remaining in darkness.

A broken radio voice stutters and asks me how I am feeling. Hissing and fizzing. Fragmented words, coming at me from multiple directions at once. I'm drunk. I'm lightheaded. More words follow—more questions, but I can't comprehend. I can't decode their meaning.

The shape shifts impatiently. A sigh, or a groan of exasperation. I twist my hands together— fingers interlocking and squeezing, a tingling sensation spreading through me from my fingertips.

Head all fuzzy—full of wasps, bees, crawling

legs. Warm—too warm. I mumble something, trying to remember what happened, and all my words spilling out into the open. For a moment, I don't recognise my own voice.

The roar of waves. Television static.

zzzzzzzzzzzzzzzzzzzzzzzzzzzzzzzzzzzzzzzzzzz
zzzzzzzzzzzzzzzzzzzzzzzzzzzzzzzzzzzzzzzzzzz

Leather creaks and groans beneath me as I try to sit up. Vision just swims and swirls. I slide down again, eyes closing. I moan. I'm going to be sick.

There is more movement from the desk area. The clunky, lumbering sounds of limbs adjusting, clambering. And the zzzzzzzzzzzzzzzzzzzzzzz constantly itching, digging.

Someone is talking. That buzzing sound is a voice, droning and drilling. It could be me, just mindlessly blabbering, but I put my hands to my face and my mouth is closed. And yet it goes on and on. So it must be the shape behind the desk. It must be the doctor.

Then Pristina, her face in my mind, her figure disappearing into the room. This room.

Papers shuffled. Someone leaning back in a chair. Where is who?

A long pause. Cold now.

Who do you think you saw?

I have to leave, I have to go.

Who do you have to go to? the voice says. Do you think she is waiting for you?

She. Not just she, but she. Spat. A word full of venom and spite. The sound of that word, the sound of it twisted, distorted into a vile sneer, creeps into my head and blossoms into a buzzing, growing in intensity with each moment.

She's a suicide, isn't she? A laugh, short and sarcastic.

The buzzing in my head grows louder and louder, my ears begin to hurt. I mutter, I stammer questions that don't finish. Just words, What? Who? And the smell, the reek of surgery-clean tools, so strong now, so overwhelming.

Falling out into the corridor, a drunk man, staggering. Vision a mess, blurred, swimming. All voices and faces and mouths. Uniforms. Feeling my way along the hall, hands reaching. All the staff, all the nurses and patients, just blurs of blue and white, and it seems they don't see me. Why don't they see me?

I have to get back to her, certain now there is danger here, as she said there was. And through the mass of twisting shapes in my eyes, I see the many that is Pristina. I see her copy army gathered outside her room, a phalanx protecting her from harm. And I realise why the threat that haunts her here has not moved on her.

Those copy eyes watch me warily as I pass, blundering, almost blind, into Pristina's room. Then light, strong. I fall to my knees and throw a hand across my eyes. I'm going to be sick.

Her voice cuts through, gracefully rising above all the noise, the sizzling of my skull, and just the sound of it eases. It subdues everything. I look up and Pristina's face is all. Through the murk of my vision, she is the one clear, sharply defined feature. She is saying my name. Over and over again. The calling pulls me up, drags me off the ground. I move to the bed and her hands are cool on my face.

She looks me in the eyes. A hard stare. Intense. You know what we have to do, don't you? she says, and I nod.

In a flurry of panic we pack up Pristina's things. We are leaving this place. I can do this one thing. I can be this for her now. I look at myself in the mirror over the sink. I have just thrown up. A metallic itch. Eyes grey. I can be strong. For her.

But now these corridors move, they shudder in pulses of light, waves of sound like someone screaming far away. We begin to run, her hand in my hand. These empty hallways now, the windows shatter as we flee. We are showered in fine shards of broken glass. And the screaming—I am unsure if it is what pursues us, or if it's me, or Pristina. So much noise. So much sound now. Overwhelming. It thuds and surges. My ears hear only my staggered breathing now. We are running on the spot. We are pulling ourselves through waist-deep water.

Now shadows arc around us—millions of flapping wings. Pristina stops and looks back, and her mouth opens. I hear only the flapping sound, the chattering of teeth. Then we see it. We see him. A shape of a man. It moves. He walks. In red and indigo blinking light.

The noise crashes now, descends around us, so loud. The cracking of walls, the splitting of plaster and wood and tiled floor. The smell of.

She runs. She drags me. Her hand in my hand. She screams at me. I stagger backwards, feeling eyes, millions of eyes. Turn around, run, protect her. We flee. We are pounding feet and breath. We are escape routes.

And as we run, the hospital folding, crumbling, breaking apart into time and space, I see the copy army tearing through all that stone and render. Claws dripping in acid, eyes blazing x-rays, they burn through brick, they disintegrate this place, swallow it into their terrible bellies. Their rage annihilates. And behind us, that shape sinks back into the depths, into the swirling maelstrom of building folding into itself.

We emerge from that dust and debris, from that storm. We move into the city, into mirror buildings—tall, steel arms thrusting. Disappearing into the streets. These streets are veins, arteries feeding the concrete heart, pounding blood-people. All these buildings, all these monuments to commerce, business, money and capital. We feel their shadows as threatening as that which pursued us in the hospital, so we drift through side-streets to reach our apartment quickly, out of sight of buildings. Out of sight of eyes and windows.

Yet there is no time for us to feel safe. Pristina shivers within the rooms while I sit alone. Her army of copies fade in and out of my vision. They whirl and spin, ghosts melting through the walls, the floor, the ceiling. I dwell on the hospital, on that shape that chased us. On the dripping away into nothing of the building.

Pristina emerges from the bathroom, hair wet and slicked back. She looks different—severe, very calm. She tells me we have to leave this place. We have to leave this place now.

Now we move into a new apartment—a large, sprawling labyrinth of rooms and halls. It belongs to one of Pristina's wealthy copies—some sort of businessman, politician, or bureaucrat. It is curving white walls, polished wood flooring, chandeliers, and softly finished furniture. From the high windows I can see the whole city, a gaping wound in the earth, as black as tar. That dirty orange light that only cities bleed—it burns my eyes more and more these days, irradiating me.

Pristina seemed cold and indifferent when I questioned the need to move. Her words were short. Her lips tight. She just kept repeating that it wasn't safe. She didn't explain the reason why, or what made this new place more secure.

So we fled through the city, across the city, between the buildings and along the streets, thick with the clotting of humanity. I held Pristina's hand as we ran, feeling her cold beside me. Shadows and shapes leapt up the walls, her reflection in windows fractured into so many others, none altogether clear, always blurred. Her army followed us, always staying close to her, those grey flats arcing out from her body in gasps of traffic noise.

This new apartment is the whole top floor of a ragged black building. There was no one here when we arrived, hissing breath up several flights of stairs lit by dull yellow. I asked her where the owners were, but she didn't answer. She knew immediately where everything was. She put her things in the master bedroom, then led me to the windows overlooking the blinking city.

Through these windows now. So much neon and street lighting, like tracer. Like time travel. The city moves through space, it hovers on the skein of history—a delicate gossamer field punctuated with murder holes and the craters of ancient explosions. Pristina stands with her back to the window, looks at me with eyes sinking into darkness. I touch her face and my fingers disappear into her powder skin. She smiles and holds my hand. She leaves inky kisses on my wrist.

She says this is freedom. This is escape. I ask her what from. Anger cracks her face and she sneers, From all that, pointing to the blinking city. I thought this is what you wanted, she says. I thought this is what we wanted. I tell her that all I ever wanted was her, that everything made sense with her. She smiles, but it quickly fades.

You don't even know me.

She walks away and I stand looking out the

window. I touch fingertips to the glass, hoping that it will fall away and the pressure will suck me out into the air. I used to dream of flying as a child. Now my dreams are of falling.

These are nights of Pristina sleeping alone. Of her planning through the days, assembling her reports and news of the massing army and her war. These are nights of me wandering the rooms and halls of this place, through the dark, searching for something. I don't know what.

These rooms swirl. They twist in a fabric of greys, cut through with streaks of glowing amber. She moves in that shimmer. She walks this apartment, calling all her ghosts to her, all her copies, her replicas. Those degrading photocopy people. That army of one.

I feel them only as a wind, as an invisible jostling. Sometimes I hear voices, many speaking at once. From Pristina's room they call and shout, angry, violent words. When I run to her, breathless in panic, I find only her, sitting upright on her bed, papers and cut-out pictures sprawled around her in a mess. She looks at me and smiles.

I can never sleep in any of the many bedrooms that burrow deep into the apartment. They grow dimmer and colder the further they go. The first few have large windows overlooking the same cityscape. Progressively, the windows become smaller, more square, like the openings in cells. The very last rooms, in almost complete darkness, so cold it makes my skin sting, the touch of frost on the walls. They have no windows.

Like freezer lockers, these cells in the deepest regions of the apartment slap my own voice back to me. Barked calls reverberate against these walls and I rub my arms to stay warm. But these are the places that Pristina's army won't go. They don't follow me down here into the dark and the cold. I hear their many voices as one, raging far, far behind me. Those words echo along concrete corridors, through the vast maze of rooms, each wall rendering every word more and more inhuman, until the sound that reaches my ears is nothing more than a crash of water over a cliff.

I huddle alone in the room at the end of the building, the coldest, darkest place I have found. I am hiding here. From Pristina. From her army. I wonder if they are hunting me through this place. I wonder if she has brought me here to play out some cruel chase through the many rooms and corridors.

I pull blankets from beds and wrap myself in them, hoping to vanish into the walls or the floor, to become stone and concrete and not be found here. Those voices though, they are always there and I have to question whether I am hearing them at all, or if it is some kind of tinnitus. I press my head to the floor, the chill burning through my skin making me gasp. For a few moments there is nothing but my breath, the pounding of my own hot blood. Then, slowly, I hear it. I hear them. I hear the shrill of their singular voice. I hear their scream tearing through the stone.

And each night in that room alone—a nightmare of colour. I sleep but don't rest. I close my eyes and see the world torn asunder. I see a fire raging, buildings reduced to rubble, swallowed up by an enormous lipless mouth, a rent in the sky that sucks everything in its wake. Rays of violet surge across the city, incinerating men, women, and children, searing the skin from their backs. All are ground down to dust. All are ash and broken bone, churned over and dug down into the earth of what I see now is a huge flat field.

Each morning I move through the maze of corridors, shivering, the stone walls slick with fine frost. I seek her out in her room, and she lies there, asleep and peaceful. I go to her, stroke her hair as I used to. She moans, her body curled up, and her lips wet. I smell cinder in the air. I lean to her, smell the char on her skin, in her hair. Her fingertips, blackened and sooty.

Sometimes I will curl up beside her and just watch her sleep. Sometimes, when her copies are moving around and agitated, I leave her and stand looking out at the city. Here and there smoke rises from places. Television news occasionally talks of fires, explosions. Mysterious structural failures.

When Pristina wakes, she sets to work scanning the news channels. She collects newspapers and pours over the headlines, cutting out stories, circling words, pictures. More and more is added to the growing mass of material she has collected, spread out on her walls. It begins to take up space in other rooms—they become her war centres, her planning spaces.

She points to a picture here of a burning office building. Here to a story about a successful business gone bankrupt. She smiles at me. She tells me how well the war is going. She tells me they are going to crash the economy, bring it all down. I stare at her desperately, longing for the days when it was just her and me.

Pristina sits astride me, she kisses me softly. I feel the warmth of her body against mine. Yet I taste the fire, the smoke, the ink that surges within her. I ask her if she really needs me, does she really want me anymore.

She looks hurt. Her hands on my face, she pulls
me close, and we are one again. She whispers
my name over and over, her fingers in my hair.
Her lips touch my neck. Her breath.

There are days of headaches. Of nosebleeds, ringing ears. The constant nightmare flushes as I sleep, the reverberations of the copies screeching down the concrete corridors. I am twisted bedding and body. I lie in the dark and the cold while Pristina and her army wage war. Alone, the flashing of lights in my eyes, the noise—the hissing, seething white noise. I fall to my knees, blood gushes from my nose. I spit, cough, spatter the bare floor in black-red. Sometimes I wake with a start, throat full of blood and vomit, and in the dark I retch and choke, clawing fingers against stone.

It's as if my body is reacting to the dreams, to the images that haunt me. Or some kind of seasickness, brought on by severe disorientation—the noise, the cold, the dark. Sometimes while I lie awake at night, I hear the sound of Pristina screaming as another of her copies degrades away while she is ghosting with them. I know she will be lying there weeping into her pillow, alone. I should go to her, but I don't.

I wander the city, avoiding the high places, the business places, the corporate steel and mirror places. I know these are her targets, and when I come close to those districts, I can smell the hot burn of sulphur, and my eyes start to sting and stream from the heat and the grit filling the air

There are parts of this city where no one goes. The buildings here are old, one hundred years or more in places, yet the modern shops and offices usually occupy only the ground and first floors. There is a huge amount of unused space above the city, in the abandoned rooms and halls that have been closed off, used as storage, or simply forgotten about. I sit and look up at this lost city—windows boarded up, overgrown, burned out, while below all is shiny new and polished.

I wonder what it's like up there. I wonder what it's like to exist in a place no one knows about, that no one thinks about. To haunt a vast, empty city, one that mirrors our own but is run down, degraded. I wonder about the freedom that must exist in a place like that.

I am wrenched back by the sound of a reversing lorry. And here I sit. In the choking, throttling grip of go-nowhere roads and tower block car parks. Offices running on sublimated hope. The city sickness like jet lag under false daylight, a shirt splattered in photocopied blood, black and crusty as crude oil suffocating sea birds on a beach made of ash.

We live inside a folding. Inside a coil of reality. Life normally moves too slowly for us to notice, but when we spin—when we feel ourselves slam hard against the walls, we can feel the reverberation. Sense the rhythm of things. Sometimes in the apartment, I put my face to the cold wall and just listen, feel, hands flat against the stone. And there it is—a soft thrum. Constant. Low. When I lie in bed all I hear is my own tinnitus—that constant squeal, like traffic noise or industrial clamour. I begin to miss the gentle pulse of reality. The quivering of the universe.

And when I lie flat on the floor, my whole body shivers to that sound. And in those moments I see the twisting and churning of space and time. I see the worlds within worlds, and it's like I'm falling through them all.

My doctor has the way of a badly tuned television—all fuzzy and incoherent. He phases in and out—a bad signal in a built up area. His voice is a foreign language dubbed into poor English. I blink sweat as I try to listen, as I try to keep up. His words run away with him, moving faster than his mouth, an awkward rent in his face that stammers and stutters, twitches. He is a sad man hiding inside a uniform.

This was Pristina's idea. I didn't want to come. I didn't want to leave the apartment. But she saw the blood, she saw me yell, hands to my head as the pain raged like a million biting insects in my skull. I think I passed out. Or maybe I simply fell asleep, there, on the floor, in her arms, exhausted. That was somewhere I usually felt safe, but now feel a great confusion about.

I chew my fingernails. I chew my lips.

I talk to the doctor for what feels like hours. Long hot hours. Dirt leaches through my skin under the glare of those surgery lights. He asks me about insomnia, about nosebleeds, stress, anxiety. He asks me about tinnitus. He talks to me about sleeping pills, about fluoxetine, citralopram, mirtazapine, trazodone, diazepam. He writes lots of scrawling sentences across crumpled paper in blue ink.

He nods and sniffs his running nose.

I talk without really being aware of what I am saying. Sweating, clenching my fists. I can feel my shirt clinging to my back. My mouth moves around embarrassed words. I talk about Pristina. I ramble in a way that must surely seem unstable. Armies. I talk about armies, and the doctor stares at me for a long time.

A cloying, uncomfortable moment. A moment of false daylight and nylon carpet.

I find I can say nothing more. My lips seem glued shut—gummed up. The sweat on my back moves in shapes, crawls across the skin. I stare at the doctor staring at me. He doesn't move. He doesn't speak. He is caught in the frame.

And the silence of this moment is washed aside by the waterfall noise in my head, gushing forth, that wall now of wailing, of screaming, of Pristina's copy army roaring all at once.

He moves forward sharply and shines a light in my eye. He asks about the tinnitus—how loud, how often, any pain? When did it start? He asks that over and over.

When did it start?

Flicking that light across my eyes.

When?

I smell him then. Beneath the sweat and the stale coffee there is the reeking of soaps and disinfectants. The scrubbing of hands and arms in scalding water running pink. The chemical process of sterilising surgical tools.

That warm running. Out of me—that red dripping from my nose. I sniff and taste the harsh rust in my throat. I cough. My hand, pale and shaking, goes to my nose to wipe, to pinch, to hold back the flow, increasing. My heart thumps in my chest, arteries are throbbing, the heat is building. In my head—the roaring, that sonorous rage.

The doctor—he cries out like a child. Falling backwards against his desk, his knees go weak and he faints for a few seconds, eyes flickering. I snatch some tissues from the desk, my hands all red and sticky blood, drying fast now in the hot office. Some has fallen on the nylon carpet. I sit and stare at the stain as I hold the tissues to my bleeding nose. I watch it become black.

The doctor awakens with a high pitched scream caught in his throat. His bloodshot eyes glare at the stain on the floor, at the blood on my hands, at the red flow stemmed from my nose by clots of white tissue. His mouth stretches, thin skin like gum, a gaunt figure of a man contorting himself into shapes of evasion. His hands reach out, he waves, he throws fingers at me. His open mouth, of crashing cars and highway murders, that noise, that terrible blackness that gets larger and larger, his hands throwing angles to the door.

So now I run from that place. I run from the doctor and that enveloping maw that seems to want to crack open his face, to grow and spread. Something deep inside me feels as though being dragged into that rent, swallowed and consumed. I can feel it slowing me as I flee through streets, the faces of people blurring together into one, into his, the face of my doctor.

Through the streets so familiar to me, now a labyrinth of dark corners and threatening concrete overpasses. I pause to check the flow of red from my nose, aware of eyes watching me. The raging in my head, those screams now have died back, given way to a relief of silence that feels awkward. I stand in a street as if in a bubble. My legs grow heavy and I begin to slide to my knees, dirty water soaking up my trousers, hands steadying myself on the ground. My head is full of bees. My head is alive with crawling and clicking.

His voice cuts through clear like chemical cleansers in filthy water. I feel it course down my spine, making my joints lock up. I see those faces around me, the slow motion eyes and mouths moving through millennia, jaws working, teeth flashing. Those tongues form sounds, those lips. A crowding round of shifting shapes, of bodies shimmering in the glow of city light flashing from mirror buildings. They speak with a singular voice, a grinding of concrete, a crushing up of roads and bridges and office buildings. It reverberates back through time, into the past.

I feel a burning desire within that great stomach, the belly that sits at the end of that throat, that mouth, that wound in his face. Fire churns within him. Ageless and terrible. He is a devourer. I see the threat Pristina felt but was too terrified to speak of. I see it made flesh. I see it in the form of a man. I see it making a mockery of a man shape.

Into weeks of war. Into months of economic decline and social disorder. Pristina's copies are business leaders and bankers. City officials, politicians, radicals. Terrorists. They find a fertile source of resentment and anger, and they poke at it like a child thrusting a stick at a rabid dog.

Into weeks of mass media news. This is where we witness the damage, the battle-scars on the world. The financial ruin. I scan the channels across three separate television screens. Through day and night, washed in that flickering light, the sometimes-static of dead air channels. Pristina directs her copies, lying in her room, eyes moving behind their closed lids. Left, right, spasmodic jerks of the hands. The occasional frozen-blood scream, and the warmth of my arms as I go to her.

I am part of this war now. Part of the revolution because now we know what hunts us. At Pristina's side I can be there when she needs me. For as much protection as her army provides her, they cannot offer the warmth of another body. The comfort of a lover's words. They are cold and amorphous, they slip in and out, here and there. And they are steeled for the fight.

I scan the channels, recording and noting down the signals, the impacts. A library of videotapes grows, detailing the struggle, from early skirmishes to the large conflicts now brewing. I sometimes record over the tapes of major victories, to further degrade our enemy. When a small financial institution is fined for breaching regulations, I tape the same story from other news channels over it, again and again and again. The final recording is grainy and fractured, the audio broken. The company collapses—bankrupt, sowing market instability that slowly begins to spread.

We are disease-spreaders. Unleashing a virus into the world. We watch it take root. We watch it infect everything.

Soon everything is disintegrating, as though under acid rain, wearing everything down, washing all the colour and substance away. The city becomes greyer. Thin. I wonder what it would take the cause the fabric to tear.

I tell Pristina about an idea I've had to begin videotaping the city from the windows. She immediately understands the implications. She laughs and dances and kisses me, her eyes on fire. I bask in the glow of her praise, wanting to please her more and more. I smile for the first time in a long time.

I position multiple video cameras at various windows of the apartment, overlooking the city from different angles. I let them record the panoramic views—of the surrounding neighbourhood, the financial district in the distance, the towers of apartment buildings, the streets below, the blinking of lights, the skies of rolling cloud—until the tapes are full. I swap them around, and record over the footage from a different view. I repeat this process over and over again, for days, weeks, using the same tapes. The process degrades the images rapidly, all colour erased, nothing but monochrome images of city, jumping, hissing, static-streaked video.

The city outside the windows becomes more unreal as these nights go by. Less a city, more a watercolour painting. We stand and watch as the rain washes it away, leeching the green of trees, the red of brick, the brown of earth. The streets run with the filth of dissolving, the waste of this place. I see it frothing at the sewers and drains, a thick putrid fat, oily and slick. I imagine it reeks of the sweat and foul shit of this city. The concentrated failure.

This apartment is walls of maps and notes and photographs. It is newspaper cuttings and the photocopied face of Pristina. The two of us move around in this warren of rooms and corridors with purpose. We are directed towards a goal now, and as much as I am unsure of our destination, I know it will be at her side, where I want to be.

I suggest that I should be copied too, like she is. Then we would be doubled—we could grow two armies. She looks at me for long moments, as if trying to decide if I am serious or not. I tell her I mean it, that I want to be at her side completely. I want to be like she is.

And she throws her arms around me, squeezing so hard it makes me gasp. She says nothing, and all I hear is the hiss of televisions and the hum of machines. Outside traffic. An airplane drones overhead.

Finally she lets go and stares out of the window. She says no, and before I can ask why—before I can insist—she tells me that there's no need.

This night a scream startles me from my sleep. A violent shrieking, a thrashing in the bed next to me. Pristina lies tangling and twisting, her hands lashing out and clawing. I back away from her coiling body of limbs. Exhaustion slows my reactions, and in those moments, another screaming, a shock of white noise and flickering red light.

I snatch at her wrists—hold her. I push her to the bed, like so many times before, in moments in passion. Now I pin her down, her mouth weeping black. Her jaw snaps shut.

Calling her name into her face. Into the darkness. She struggles on the bed beneath me, and I fight to keep her still. To stop her harming herself.

We huddle in the pale light of the city. Around us lie videotapes, televisions, their screens all stuttering of static. A blanket wraps around her shoulders and she shivers. Her hair is soaked and matted about her face and head, her shoulders. I take a cloth and wipe her brow. She flinches, eyes wide in alarm.

I coax and beg her to tell me what happened, but she sits there staring into the hissing television screens. I hear her teeth chattering, but when I try to hold her, to warm her, she pulls away sharply.

I sit with her through the remainder of the night. We drink hot, sweet tea, and gradually the silence between us retreats and she moves close to me, whispering about her childhood, something she has never spoken of before.

She is running through a forest, autumn-damp and mouldering. She is young, and she is playing with someone. Her breath falls in gasps of freezing cloud, and her skin tingles in the air. She has been playing hide and seek with friends, but she thinks she is lost now, blind amongst the trees and undergrowth, branches that seem to reach out and snare her.

Feet sink into soft earth as she runs through the woods. Colours melt and blur on the periphery. The shapes of trees and undergrowth lose definition, seem to bleed together. Strange, disturbing images suggest themselves. Young eyes exaggerate the unknown, imaginations fuelled on fairy tales and ghost stories, piece together monsters.

Silver trees with peeling bark, leafless, scarred black and brown. She runs into the distance, disappears into the tangled mass of green and brown, where the faces and eyes and mouths lurk.

Glimpses of the grey sky through the tree tops, running. Pressure of the air tightens. Ground so cold, winter betraying its encroaching menace with pin pricks on skin. The chill seeps through her clothes, lost and alone, awaiting the advance of monsters all around, circling in predatory glee.

Ancient stone bones erupt. Trees peel back, the legs of the forest opening up to reveal the hidden secrets within, as the pathway before her appears, leading her eyes to the rotting hulk of the old hospital building. They told her witches had died here, rolled from the tower on top of the hill in a barrel. Built on their ashes, they said. Built from their bones.

She walks slowly through the trees, bursting roots snatching, branches ensnaring, a fine mist of rain beginning to fall. The stench of damp. Great waves of rotting undergrowth roll over the forest floor, crashing around ancient tree trunks, banks of exposed earth like cliffs. Malodorous brown-orange reeking ocean of decomposition. Peeking through the surface of this sea, the bones of fallen branches jut, suggesting limbs of long dead murder victims, arms outstretched in yearning.

Woodland brown bleeds away into hospital grey, sun-baked green walls, peeling yellow paint over faded white wallpaper. Broken tiled floor, leaf-strewn, rubbish of beer cans, old fires and teenage sex. Washed with dirt, the encroachment of the forest into the building. Slowly the stone and timber will return to the earth.

Stepping over broken masonry with the thumping of blood through veins loud in her ears. Shoes skidding on dusty floors above, laughter, and someone running away. She calls out weakly, voice lost in the darkness, absorbed by the damp, faded-white walls.

The smell inside worse than in the decaying woods. The hint of something else, something that pushed itself through from another time. The dank flooring, the rotten timbers and the peeling paint, but the scent of something older.

She calls out again, but her voice is travelling through more than just the air, masonry dust and paint chips. It falls flat and wooden against the damp-damaged walls, plaster falling away like ancient dry skin, huge scales of an ageless dragon. And as she moves further into the increasingly dark interior, she becomes more aware of descending into some enormous maw, the tract of some creature's gut.

The dust hangs heavy in the air and fills her lungs with the weight of years. Scattered claw-like shadows burst from corners, grow up walls, a spreading darkness over faded white.

Now dark, musty corridors give way to bright, sterile wards, fluorescent strips line the ceiling, flickering in time with her thundering heart. A moment of lag in her step. The air seems to grow heavy. She slides into a few frames of slow motion. Then the chatter of conversation and phones ringing at the nurses' station surges her back into normal time. The buzz of visiting hour. The sickly sweet hanging in the air.

Now standing in a ward, six beds, three on each side, all occupied with elderly patients. She looks down at herself, sees the uniform, the white and blue of the nurse. Friends and family of patients are arriving, sitting by beds, handing out gifts of flowers and fruit. Her ears roar.

She turns and steps into the corridor, nearly walking into another nurse. Disorientated, she hears someone talking to her, only they aren't using her name. The man steps closer, but his words seem to get further away.

Pristina looks into his face and screams.

She sleeps. Around her the televisions hiss and hum—flickering guardians of static. Like her copies they shift and blink. Colours of light wash across her body while I watch. The stillness of the apartment. I reach across and put my hand to her head. She sweats. Slick and grimy. Her body, that silent flat field, undulates rhythmically with the sound of televisions. The beating of her heart jars with my own, a furious pounding of drums, the frequency getting lower, and lower.

I wonder if she is asleep or pretending to be dead.

Pristina's dream unnerves her. For days I ask her to explain it—to tell me if it was a memory of something or just a nightmare.

There is nothing to tell, she says, looking away towards the windows. I see her face reflected in the glass. She ghosts. For a moment that image flickers, and I see—I don't know what I see.

Now nightly this tormented screaming, this horror show. Sometimes I fall into her room and red light arcs from her mouth like the rust of blood, and her body throws shadows in wild contortions. Now the aftermath of all this thrashing, in the glow of hissing televisions, their gentle rock and hum. Her body throbs next to mine, shivering in the cool of the night. She mutters and whispers as she drifts through sleep, and I am reminded of those days in our old apartment, those days before the army, before the war, when it was only the two of us.

I wish sometimes to talk while she sleeps. I wish to tell her something comforting, something true. My mouth works awkwardly in the dark, and shapes form. My tongue moves. Lips are dry and words take no form. The air remains empty, silent. Just the hush of television calmly rolling over us both—an ocean of static.

Memories, my past, all reel through like old

film. Click-clacking, machines lumbering. Something to tell her, to whisper in her ear as she sleeps. Something about me—who I am, what I am.

There is nothing to tell. There is nothing there.

Nothing matters though. Not anymore. None of it. I am what this world has made me. I am grey and wasted, barely living. Now pushed, now beaten, ignored. Now fighting.

Her body is nothing as I carry her to the bedroom. She is air. She is mist of clothing and black hair. I lay her pale against the bedspread, and she moans and curls. Pristina is a battlefield, a worn landscape of scars and trenches, tripwires and traps. I used to enjoy navigating those dangerous pathways. She would laugh knowingly. She would twist and rise up. She would hold me.

Now the televisions flicker and noisily spit into faces talking. They speak of murder, of many victims left butchered. They show dead faces in a monochrome pornography.

And Pristina opens her eyes to stare at the screens. And she points.

Murders move across this city in great scars—
light trails arcing back and forth.

Every night now, with every low pass of the
sun and the dawn of the moon, this killer stalks
the streets, reaches out and finds another.
Blood mists the air. Falls as rain. People talk
in hushed voices of screams heard down
alleyways, of a dark figure in long coat and tall
hat. A night phantom.

Newspapers fill with the lurid details, the
sensational headlines. Television crews talk to
people on the streets, about the butcher, the
doctor, the surgeon, the veterinarian. About
the man from hell who slaughters in the night.

And I see his face in my dreams. I see his
face on the television screen, in the static of
dead channels—a burst of flies. I stand at the
windows and see his shape cutting through the
streets below, hunting for her, but finding only
fakes. His rage ricochets through alleyways,
slapping against the glass before my eyes. In
those moments I feel his thunder. His thirst.

Pristina never leaves her room. She huddles in
there alone, afraid of being discovered, feeling
the loss of every victim as though it were a
piece of her that were being cut away. And I
know that that is exactly what is happening.
Each murder is a part of her gouged out. It's

as if she feels the knife stabbing and slashing herself. I wonder if I examined her body, would I find her a battlefield of wounds?

Despite this she demands to know the news. She still wants the newspapers, and the televisions turned on. She wants to know about each new incident. Every kill. She knows them all intimately, and as the reports come in each morning, she writes a name down on a growing list.

And here I am powerless to protect her. She remains as withdrawn as before, and I wander through these rooms alone, her army of copies in hiding as the red blanket of murder smothers the city.

The war is put on hold, and Pristina sinks into a depression. Only when she is fighting is she happy. Only when full of the rage, the hot blood of battle, does she smile and hold me close to her. During these days, these weeks of murder, she hides from her pursuer, and from me, as though I am the one who hunts her.

What would you have me do? I ask her. And although she doesn't say it, I know she is thinking that this is my fault. I was the one who exposed her in the hospital. I was the one who allowed that creature to find her. She is thinking that if only I had left her in the bathtub.

I spend days roaming the city alone. In search of someone, maybe something. Something that might not even exist.

And so I leave Pristina in the apartment, alone. She asks me where I go each day, pleads with me. She is worried I am leaving her. I insist I am not, and she looks unconvinced. And there is a part of me that wonders that perhaps I am. That I am seeking a way out through some kind of confrontation. My destruction. The murderer that haunts the city has put us on the defensive. Rather than attacking, pushing the war forward, we are holding back. Too terrified to risk exposure and slaughter.

I know the danger in walking these streets. The thing that is cutting down the copy army will seek me out as well. With every step I take I feel as though eyes are watching me. As though the scent of my blood gives me away, and somewhere in the dark, terrible jaws await.

I move through the crowds of people, their eyes seem to linger on me for too long. I turn and look at a woman who pushes by me, for a moment seeing a flicker of recognition in her face. She is walking away from me. Her back flat. My heart pounds. I breathe.

Hands in front of my face shaking. My body sticky hot and sweating. A terrible closeness all around me. The city folding down all around me.

It's as if I want to be found. As if I am walking out into this minefield, arms out wide, calling to the creature that stalks this city and declaring Here I am, come and take me.

Such callous disregard. Such stupidity. I shouldn't make a mistake like this. That's what Pristina would say. Her command of her own battleground now so strong, her awareness of every city space so complete. The map she has in her head, across her walls, of newspapers and magazine articles, black and white and full colour glossy pages, lines and chalk, and blood and ink and sweat and the constant rhythm of her own heart beating in time with the city and the breath of the people. And I stagger around here blind. A child. Naively searching for what? To prove myself maybe. To be worthy.

And this city made a slaughterhouse. A labyrinth of murder. It reeks of blood drying on filthy tenement walls. The sweat of fear leaching into polyester shirts. I wonder if it is me and put my hand up to my face, a sudden sense of panic that I'm bleeding.

I'm crying. Somehow without even realising, I have started sobbing uncontrollably in the middle of the street. Tears. Snot. I snatch at the air with my teeth. No one is even looking at me anymore.

A fracture in time, bleeding, seeping into everything. We scan road maps and find murders highlighting a route, pointing a way towards something as yet unknown. A death vector that burns, sears on the page. We smell the acrid stench in our sleep. A smouldering like a hidden fire deep underground in a seam of peat.

And I remember breathing. Brilliant white light, harsh like those hospital lights you see when you're dying. My eyes stinging. Just breathing. Then the thunderous rumble, cracking concrete. My blood. My life.

And I remember her breathing against me. Her body heaving beneath me. Skin cold as she gasped, eyes fixed on mine. Her writhing, twisting shapes. Oil on water. Black tar clinging. The shrill squawk of animals drowning.

And I remember that begging, questioning stare.

Where were you?

Movement coils through indigo beams. He steps forward—a coughing cloud of filth, a suffocating blanket that envelopes everything in its wake. And that sound. Frenetic, distant, but approaching. The sound of a machine drilling, tearing, devouring. The sound of something inhuman consuming. The eyes of my doctor cut through grease and vomit smeared across a windscreen. His mind a twisted maelstrom of surgery and shapeless words, muttering and stammering. Such lunatic intent. Unfathomable mindlessness.

The cracked face of the doctor stares out of the mirror, lips curled in a cruel bureaucratic grin, all filing cabinets and blue ink piss. His mouth moves incoherently around flaccid sounds, tongue lolling, saliva coated chin. The cold murder stare. Masturbating in the surgery office. Dead fish eyes, staring out of the depths of the bath tub, overflowing, black water rushing across a white tiled floor where I lie bleeding red and black into a white cotton shirt.

He stands in a shimmering blue light, a figure glitching in space and time. He flickers. You blink and he's gone. You blink and there he stands, a frozen shape caught in a moment of visceral reality. He moves through an apartment of ancient yellow walls, broken, crumbling with age. These rooms are as old as the earth. They grew out of the dirt with the massive trees of timeless forests. His eyes glimmer with the chemistry of polluted oceans—an oil slick glistening under a foreign sun, consuming sea birds and destroying beauty spots. He scans the rooms with infra-red, ultraviolet, x-rays, cutting through plaster and concrete and brick. No depth to those hollows. No idea of the eye itself. Only the quick cuts of images—the leather of hospital restraints, the creases in uniforms.

He tears through our old apartment. He blasts those ancient walls with black matter from his gaping mouth—an eruption of flies, crawling insects, twisting worms. His rage burns everything around him. The building blackens through the brick. Steel and iron glow bright red and orange. And when he stands before the mirror, for a moment he is reflected as an ash cloud pouring down the side of a volcano. Then the glass distorts, buckles—cracks and shatters into thousands of shards.

Our abandoned belongings—clothes, books, the odd photograph. His hands move over them, as careful as a nervous lover. He touches fingers to our flat photograph faces and the picture smoulders. He forces his finger through the burning hole in her face. He shivers.

A shadow floating through curtains of flame.

An absence of something. He emerges from the burning building and brushes ash from his suit.

Around us the vast hospital is dying. A decaying monolith of a long dead idea. A hope. A dream. And the stench of that death, that ruin and failure, hanging in the air as a fog, sticking to our clothing and skin. I can smell it in Pristina's hair as we sleep, huddled in corners of rooms, breathing the damp air.

Forever those neon eyes, killer beams of indigo cutting through walls on an endless search pattern. Wave after wave of pursuit through barren rooms, patients mere memories imprinted into furniture, floors, bedding—just shadows against walls.

And when he moves with such intent, the doctor burns a trail of cold shit in his wake. He knows her. He can smell and sense her presence. And he is a cough. He is a thick glob of red-brown copper. A smeared smile. Lips curling into a broad surgery grin.

And so we move through the body of the hospital. We exist within the invincible sound of its body. Its breathing. We are awake, not living, not dying, merely waiting. Bloodshot eyes and wide open. Some nights the pain burns the pit of my stomach, down through my legs. And Pristina crying, dragging me by the arms, screaming at me to stand, to walk, to help. And all I am is a collapse of arms and legs, bent double, on my knees, screaming into the indigo light.

Images flicker and repeat in these unconscious moments. Soundless fragments. And a cool sweat, entangled by bedding, the sudden panic of restraint. Then the calming hands. The whisper. Then her body warm and close. Wrapped around her, as outside the rain lashes the curtainless windows.

I dare not move. A warm body provides little security now. And she as troubled, as damaged. Yet all I can do is pull her closer, hold her tighter. Curling together into an unheard song.

The stream of images as torrential as the rain. Of bathtubs, collapsing towers, buried beneath piles of concrete.

He is painted with lipstick and blood. He flickers all along the highways, blinking out a hateful, rage-filled pattern. The doctor stands knee-deep in the excrement of a world sold short on tabloid dreams, all shiny and glossy with the pornographic smiles of lips and teeth.

He wears his suit of cheap polyester, interwoven with the newspaper cuttings of his victims, stitched together with the hair of nervous first time lovers, shot in the backseats of their cars. The lonely highway stalker, chasing down drivers with a machete and a revolver. Dark nights of blood spatter and cigarettes ground under heels in laybys lit by flickering neon.

His map is tattooed on his chest, in blue typewriter ink, plotting his course through memory and history, his never ending search and his chase. His hunt. It sweats through his pores in dark rivulets of surgery signatures and prescription labels, the dosage always excessive. You can see him sometimes sucking on his blue-bleeding fingers, slowing his own time, shifting out of sync with the world, moving backwards into the past.

The doctor steps from a doorway, from hell into darkness. In the building behind him a light flickers. Brilliant white flashes, revealing a scene of butchery. Of slaughter. Of art. He moves through the streets, his veins pulsing with the narcotic power of satisfaction. And yet he feels the hunger still, deep inside him. An always unsated ravenous desire. A need to push on. To kill. To find her.

He wipes blood from his mouth, staining shirt cuffs. His hellish nightmare of a face. An ever shifting, swirling morass of flesh.

So lost in the memory of another. Leaning hard against the cold, tiled wall as blood begins to seep from my nose, gather on my top lip. Feeling the dizziness. Tasting the metallic itch. Sounds of slaughter.

In the silence of the apartment, Pristina lies sleeping. She is at peace—at least that's how it seems. Dreaming, ghosting. And yet here I stand, sweating and shivering, blood streaming now from my nose, my face, the sensation of something black crawling out of my mouth. And a scream caught. Hands over my mouth—my hands, his hands, whose fucking hands. And a smell of something rotting, decaying, a corpse buried in the walls. Then Pristina on the bed surrounded by bloodied sheets, a torrent of red gushing from within her to arc across the walls. Then the world spinning, and I know I'm falling back. The ceiling becoming the floor. I catch the wall behind me, and everything becomes a blur, everything is under the ocean and the roar and crash of the waves are above.

So I sink.

So I drown.

The people in this hospital aren't real. They walk the corridors in uniforms, white coats, blue overalls. They reek of soap and coffee. They move their mouths and words pour out like clouds of flies. I watch them write things down on charts, their fingers leaking blue ink. Spreading stains in the pristine polyester fabrics. But underneath it all they are empty. They are nothings.

Night comes and night goes, each time replaced by the weak suggestion of light, pushing its way through thin curtains by my bedside. No matter how often this happens, and I've lost count of the days that have passed, I still squint my eyes, as though just released from some subterranean prison. Or maybe I'm just afraid of what each morning will bring.

There is a doctor who visits me. He asks questions in a voice so indistinct it may as well not even be real. I don't answer. I don't look at him.

He writes words down in a blue scrawl. I hear him sigh—breathe hard. He stands by the window and the pissy light of day swirls around him, arcing oddly. I try to see his face for a moment but am blinded. I just want to sleep.

Let me sleep.

Let me sink.

In darkness there is release. And there are dreams. There is a terror. A sound that begins very far away, and slowly builds, surging up with a sickening amber light. I am drowning. I am full of thick red bleeding, scrambling. I am clawing and snatching.

Upwards out of water and into my bed. The sweat runs from my body. Sheets tangle my limbs.

These nights I cry and try not to sleep. These nights I wish for her. Whisper her name into my bed clothes.

Each day a nurse takes me to see the psychiatrist, a man who reminds me of my own doctor. I sit in his office and remember when I sat in the office of Pristina's doctor. How the panic seared through me. How we fled from that place, together, hand in hand. How we began to fight back.

And yet here you are, he says to me, some kind of doubtful smile. There is no war. There are no ghosts. His eyes seek me out and I am too tired to fight him.

His voice drains me of will. Each day, each visit to his room, I grow more and more weary.

I mumble wordless sounds. Some days I open my mouth and no sound emerges. Just breath. Empty rasps of air.

I blink and he is just a blur.

Some days the nurse takes me to sit in the gardens after the sessions. We sit together in the sun. She talks to me about mundane things. I stare into the distance. I stare through walls.

These days become merely questions. Each new day is a new topic for interrogation. It starts with me. He wants to know my name and where I'm from. I think I've already told them my name. I might have invented one, or made a meaningless sound, like static—zzzzzzz. Just a glitching, stuttering machine, like the monstrous things that Pristina works with, spitting out imperfect copies of words, smeared and smudged by my mangled metal lips.

And they want the know what happened to me. They want to know how I came to be unconscious in the street, how I ended up leaning against a railing babbling incoherently, grabbing people by their collars and barking, eyes red and wild.

I have no memory of those events. I suspect they never happened, that they are lying to me. Twisting my mind against me. Everything before the hospital is a fog. Pristina's face lurches in and out of the gloom of watery images, sometimes sharply in focus, and sometimes lost amongst the wash of colour— an abstract painting.

I remember my first day here, when medicated I was led through the maze of corridors to my room. The kind of room where the door has no handle on the inside. They fix a plastic band around my wrist. I look at it, sitting on the leather chair in the dim office. Fingers trace over the lettering. I say each letter out loud in turn. A question from the doctor. I pull my sleeve over the band, ashamed or afraid of giving something away.

He tells me that there are police who want to question me. About murders.

About a wave of red seeping across the city. About bodies found butchered in doorways, alleys, homes, and parks. About faces slashed and broken open. About a city reverberating to the sound of a single scream, pushing up from under the concrete, through the stone walls and the steel and glass.

And my hand held out before me starts to shake. I can't control it. I feel something wet dripping from my nose, and stare at the floor between my feet as a blotch of red starts to grow. And grow. And grow.

I hear the doctor's voice calling to me, or to someone else, as I kneel on the floor, my blood still running free. My hands move through the spreading puddle, my fingers push through that thick red, moving it, spreading it. Shaping. And I see. I can see there, within the black-red—her face. Pristina's face. She is reaching to me. She is within me still. She is calling out.

Bloody hands and face, I am taken away by a pair of orderlies. Their white uniforms streaked and smeared in red they resemble butchers—murderers. And I start to yell. To struggle. I reach out to the walls, those flat helpless surfaces, nails raking hard through thin paint. And in a mass of flailing bodies, they hold me to the ground and fill me with chemicals. They restrain my body. They bind my mind.

A nurse comes to my room, patiently cleaning the blood from my hands, my face. Through the cloud of medication I recognise her as the one who normally accompanies me to the gardens. I enjoy her company. She is calming and soft. The shrill tinnitus caused by the drugs in my veins begins to move into the background, to lower in pitch, down and down, until it is a subsonic throbbing. A pulsar in space.

She encourages me to cooperate with the doctor's questions. To tell them my name—my real name. Help them to help me.

I write my name over and over on hospital notepaper with a soft child's crayon. They won't let me have a pen or pencil. The words are smeared on the page as my hands move over them, my fingers becoming stained. Gradually the words degrade further and further down the page, they smudge into one another, ceasing to form anything resembling actual words. I repeat them out loud, trying to find my way back into my name. But my voice descends into guttural barks. The words deform in my mouth. They erode. And as I continue writing, over and over again, I finally tear through the paper, the nib of the crayon moving over the bedsheets as the words I cough up disintegrate into noise.

In sweat—I lie. Wrapped in bedding soaked through. Muttering meaningless phrases. Trying to find my voice. Trying to find my name. Pristina's face in red and black and blue, twists and coils, my hands moving through her features, distorting them. She is out there on her own. She is calling to me. She is pushing through my very blood.

The sessions with the psychiatrist go on. Each day, for longer and longer. I am taken from my room—a cell full of scrawled drawings and the echoes of my voice shattering against walls— to a lecture theatre where he waits. He paces. He clears his throat. I don't see his face. I won't look at him. I sit and stare at my hands. They are covered in the smeared blue-green of wax crayon. I scratch words into the wooden desk with the edge of a fingernail. Making a mark. Calling out to her.

Her name. Over and over. Carved into the soft desk surface. To reach her. To summon her vast army. Where are they now? Why don't they come for me? Why are there none of her ghosts among the hospital staff? The nurses, doctors, orderlies. Someone.

And so a prisoner here. Of this war. To be held and questioned. Surrounded by these enemies. I must not let them in. I will give them nothing of myself. I will not surrender. And I must prepare myself for torture. They will take me to dark and secret places, hidden deep inside the hospital. They will pump chemicals into my veins. They will beat me, bloody me, make me spit up bile and blood and lies.

The sun rises and the sun sets. I meet every question with silence. With a turn of the head. With my closed eyes.

Sometimes he talks about the murders. He asks if I know about them, and if I have seen the news coverage. He reads names of victims. Talks about police. Just more uniforms. He unfolds a newspaper and spreads it out before me. Look, he says. And asks if I recognise the faces.

I stare at my feet. At the floor. I look for the windows and try to see sky. The sun.

His breathing heavy. Frustrated. I hear his knuckles crack.

Something in the air changes. A shift takes place. The atmosphere becomes charged, and my hair bristles. My teeth feel as though they are rattling in my jaw, and a sick amber light moves across the room.

He takes hold of my face with clinical hands. He shows me images I don't want to see. Holding them up before my eyes, holding my face in those neon-cold hands that reek of stale coffee and piss. Poorly photocopied pictures of a woman's face, oddly disfigured by the blocky black ink and reproduction distortion, as if it had been copied multiple times, again and again, until all that remained was a stain, a blotch, a mass of churning black like a living, boiling, seething lump of tar.

I don't want to look. I don't want to see. But my eyes open of their own will and I know the face I see on those pages.

He knows it too. He sits in front of me and repeats questions in a slow voice. Each word drags out over hours. Each sentence is dawn to dusk. He asks about her. He doesn't use her name.

I think.

I hear her name—but I have been repeating it over and over, inside my head. Have I been saying it out loud? My own blabbering giving her away, exposing her to him. If he knows her name, my name, then he can find her.

The doctor moves through words. He breathes in the shapes and sounds. He can follow them back to the origin. Back to the soul that spoke them and gave them life. He itches for a taste of that air. For any sense of that colour. His body arches when he feels them. And he stands before me now, his body shuddering as his hands press into the wooden desk, searing it black.

And in a rage he throws the pictures of Pristina's face down on the blackened table. The sound he makes like grinding bones. He points at her again and again, pushes my face against the grainy images. My eyes closed, but I smell the ink, the scorching wood and flesh.

An incredible shuddering moves through the floor and the walls. Everything begins to bend and distort. And I think of all the ways I have failed her, how I have left her now to fight on alone. I hope she knows I am held against my will. That I am a prisoner. The best I can do now is not lead him to her.

I close my eyes and feel the room around me fall away into space.

Hospital walls and strips of false daylight. A ceiling of cardboard. Such a cavernous monolith. And here we are taken on a guided tour through the Villa Grimaldi, Clínica Santa Lucía, Auschwitz, Lubianka, Abu Ghraib. The dull sound of a corpse falling on ice. Corridors of dirty concrete, bloodied by broken hands, sweat, and skin. Dragging. Clawing. It dries between your toes. Chokes in your throat.

So here we lie. With open mouths screaming at the windowless walls.

So here we lie. Tied to our beds and medicated. Made calm. Made sane.

The faces of doctors, over centuries, twisted by the history of all the slaughterhouses of regimes gone bad. We walk, hand in hand. You and I. Practitioner and patient. Sane and insane.

And all I see here are the cold iron bathtubs, filling with freezing water, tainted blue by chemicals. Medicines. Diamonds glint in the showers. I see her lie in the womb-like bath, gurgling, struggling, held under by invisible psychic hands. Those piercing violet eyes. Indigo bleeding through her skin.

And when I step back—all overgrown in weeds. So many decades of abandon. So many centuries of rot, sunk deep into the earth. Here I kneel and dig my hands into the soil, the dark, bloody soil. To bury myself. To burrow and sleep.

Yet these legs ache when curled up in the bed sheets, during these long hot nights, twisting and coiling. Laughing into the pillow, a hollow mocking kind of voice. You strung together a few pathetic excuses, scrawling them out on torn paper, ink stains on the corner of your mouth. And that growing pain in the joints, always stretching those muscles.

I feel unreal, I tell her. I feel made of plastic. And she smiles, head tilted awkwardly to one side, hanging from the gallows.

I know she understands without her saying anything. She just fixes me with her black hole eyes, emitting a pitch perfect B-flat, thrumming through the universe. That intense sound, vibrating, thundering in the inner ear with its low frequencies, resonating in the skull, in the spine, in the pelvis. She puts her hand to my face and her touch is ice. Freezer burn leaves marks across the furniture. The whole place reeks of melting nylon.

Pristina is a battlefield—a war fought over centuries. Her body a terrible killing ground. Wreathed in barbed wire, the searchlights of opposing factions constantly scour the surface for anyone stranded in the no-man's land of her navel. Lying beside her as she sleeps, I pick at the wounds, fingers tracing over the slick, freshly bloodied trenches of cuts. Darkened bruises on her wrists slowly turn green as the hours slip away.

The broken road like a funeral path cutting across the great expanse of the flat field. Sick yellow walls close in and we lie there together, cold concrete interrupting sleep in blunted words, the rotten teeth of the liar.

He stares out of the television. He speaks placid words made of warm orange and respectable suits. But his mouth makes the shapes of murder.

The guts of the hospital are a maze of tunnels. Dark, hidden passages that criss-cross the underground, for the transportation of laundry, machinery, beds. Some orderlies tell stories of moving bodies around in the damp and amber light. How the sound of trolley wheels on the concrete makes a scraping sound. How awkward shadows lurch across the walls—lumbering horror movie figures.

And here I wake in dark rooms, with the sound of dripping water and the stench of decay. The images flicker. They drip into a sink of cold water and dissipate—red blooms and jellyfish breath.

Here there are rooms full of jars of all sizes. The shapes of preserved human organs, body parts, foetuses. A strange glow and blinking pulses through the glass, bending into convex distortions.

I wake in a room strapped to a bench, a lump of hard rubber between my teeth. I struggle but can't free myself. The lights strobe. My body goes stiff.

Naked, stumbling through filthy narrow passages in the darkness. Gothic archways, like from some old film or book I read once. The walls slick with slime, with algae, with blood. I fall into the water that rushes, ice cold and merciless. I open my mouth to shout, call out—to scream for help. And my voice doesn't come. Instead a thick black liquid pours out of me. So I choke it up. I cough and vomit into the flow of dirty water, the sewer. The blackness tastes of rubber and plastic and the collars of nurses uniforms. Fists clench as I empty myself.

I wake and I cannot move. My eyes stare and begin to dry. No sound from my mouth as I try to shout out, to alert someone. I imagine myself struggling against some kind of restraints, but my muscles don't twitch. This body lies uselessly here, laid out on a table or a desk or the floor. I can't even blink. And inside I am screaming to someone, to anyone.

This feels like those stories you hear of people waking up during operations. Of being paralysed as they are opened up, sliced into, cut, and stitched. And all I can see is some distant ceiling, a grey slab of concrete for a sky. I try to listen and all I hear is the rushing of water—a stream, a river, a waterfall. A collapse.

And so I see myself from above, from that high ceiling, hanging there, floating maybe. I see my body laid out like a laboratory experiment. People in uniforms gathering around and exchanging discussions, pointing, and nodding. And I shout at them to leave me alone—words that fall soundlessly into the void of space. Over the cliff and into a vast crashing. I watch as they slice me open. As they open my chest and use chewed pens to point at my lungs, full of water and chemicals. They use bare hands to handle my heart, to cut it out and turn it over, examining it like you would examine a fruit. They place it in a metal dish. Dry, empty, no blood leaking.

I float high above as they empty my body of organs, as they dig me out until I am just a shell.

We walk together. Our arms interlinked. Through these gardens of green. Of bird song.

An aroma moves on the breeze. Fresh cut grass. There are men in white overalls mowing the long strips of lawn. Here the fountain flows, and we pause to sit. The sun is on your face.

The hospital casts a long shadow over the gardens. An ever shifting shape—all towers and chimney stacks rising, vast banks of windows and red brick.

I blink and it's a pristine white edifice, modern glass and steel.

I blink again and you are standing before me in your uniform. You look radiant. You are glowing. Nothing here is as bright as you or your smile. And your mouth opens and all the sound in the universe pours out in a blinding light that sears my soul.

You're talking, and I am listening, but I don't really know what it is you're talking about. Your voice fades in and out of my perception, and although I am looking into your face, all I see there is a mixture of colours. The soft suggestion of lips. The gentle wave of hair.

I sigh. I feel something itching in my veins, but I am too relaxed here to think on it for too long. The warm sunlight fills me up—I feel as though I am glowing. Are you the sun? Am I in orbit around you?

Your voice slips through the fog, and you are talking about dosages, medications, routines. I screw up my eyes. I close myself to those words. Something about them scratches my retinas. I feel my eyes water.

I blink.

We are sitting beneath a tree in the centre of an enormous field, flat black grass as far as the horizon. There are no leaves on this tree, just skinny arms that reach into the sky—a blood-red firmament stretching and blurring into nothing. You are sitting astride me, your uniform pulled roughly around your hips. Your lips are on mine.

You are breathing into me.

I am breathing into you.

I blink.

You lead me to a bench in the shade of a large gnarled tree. Branches reach out to me. They reach out to you—to snare you, to grab you and take you away. I move away from the shadows, the twisting shapes of fingers, like claws.

And then the sun moves and we are in the light again. The warmth. The heat. I'm sure these things come from you alone. You are the sun, after all. You are the only sun I have. Inside the building, the hospital, there is no sky. So I orbit you. I bask in your radiation. Blast me to dust with your x-ray eyes. Your nuclear mouth.

You're talking now, and I am listening. I don't know what the words are. You have no language. You are shape and sound and light. And I am the withered tree in your shadow. The tiny planet baked dry and barren.

These are the moments you give me. These are the garden walks you take me on to relieve the anxiety and stress caused by the doctor's constant questioning. You don't approve of his methods—I can see that in the way your brow furrows when you greet me at the door to his office. It's in the curt responses you give him.

And the way he smiles at you. The way he leers as he says your name, those lips moving so grotesquely around each syllable. The curl of a tongue.

How long have I been here? I think I ask you that every time we sit outside. But I forget what you tell me. When I return to my room, to my bed, to the tangle of sheets and the tangle of my mind, nothing else exists.

You told me that you had come here to work from a place that was torn apart by war. You could have been from anywhere. Or maybe everywhere.

Sometimes when we walk around the courtyard, amongst the chemical stonework, the grass appears blood-black, and the bird song descends into a television hiss. When I look up, I see the crows lurking on the rooftops and guttering of the monolith. And when I look into your eyes, they become bottomless rents in your pale face, sucking in light from all around. In those moments I feel hollow — the pit of my stomach becomes dry and empty.

Sometimes it's like you have no face at all.

We sit in the shade. We admire the fountain. I like the sound of splashing water, and the clean smell. I don't like getting wet. You walk me through the gardens, through the flowerbeds, and young saplings growing strong in the daylight. You pause to smell the aromas. The

colours make me dizzy. So much red. So much
red.

All red.

Spinning.

And each time you catch me. Each time you
see it coming, and you sit me down on a bench
until the fuzziness in my head has cleared. You
say something about it. You talk about it being
something to deal with. Something important.
And I know. Because each time I look down
at my feet and see a small patch of blood
spreading out from the drips that splash down
from my nose.

You encourage me to keep a diary. To write down my thoughts and feelings. It feels awkward—exposing. I don't like to reveal that much about myself. To give myself away. It's as though by doing so I will become less real. But you insist, with gentle pressure and easy whispered words during garden walks in the sun. The doctor seems to agree with this idea and so I am allowed a pencil.

My early attempts are mere scrawls. Shapes of animals and meaningless symbols. I'm so embarrassed that I abandon my garden walks for several days. I spend my time pacing my room, pushing my worn pencil tip over the walls, seeking words that connect me with the images I see each night, those that swirl in my memories and dreams.

And I wonder what Pristina would do. She would fight, of course. She would struggle and never give in to this place. Smashing walls with her voice. A language of shattering and screeching heat and sound and light.

My writing turns to warfare. To confrontation. Here I name my enemies, and declare their locations. I expose their movements and disguises. A map in words revealing the shapes of conspirators. I unmask them all—the doctor, this hospital, all these drugs and medicines and white walls. Hundreds, thousands of lines of pencil-grey handwriting, over so many ripped and torn pages

And soon words run together into streams. I pour myself out onto pages.

Soon—I can't stop.

Letters to the authorities. To the city leaders— the politicians, business leaders, police officials. I want to alert them to the danger lurking amongst them. I want them to know that they are all in danger.

You read my letters with a strange expression. Anxiety. Fear. I'm not allowed any contact with those on the outside, and so I ask you, I beg you, to take my letters to the people who need to see them. And you agree, although you seem reluctant.

You leave me in my room, writing, always writing.

Often when I am thinking of you, I am thinking of escaping. I dream of you helping me. You smuggle me out in the laundry. You disguise me as a fellow nurse. I feel my heart pound. Sweat glistens across my body.

Then the flashes of locked doors, barred windows, security guards, and all the drugs, restraints, and quiet rooms.

I wish for a great wind to tear the walls asunder. To rip this place apart. Pristina opened a void so vast it swallowed a hospital whole. Maybe I never left that building, and I have been swallowed by the same throat. And here I fall. Here I drift.

And so to anchor myself, I write. I tell them that something is stalking the city. That a creature has emerged out of hell, something completely inhuman. I tell them I have seen this monster, looked into its face, its blank, featureless eyes. I implore them to come to the hospital and arrest the doctor, that I am not safe here.

I sit so close to the television in the day room that my eyes stream. It makes the other patients angry, and the staff don't like it when patients are agitated. So I catch glimpses when I can. Between game shows and soap operas. Between the random static of dead air channels and bad reception, commercials full of lips and teeth, primary colours that burn through the screen.

I wait for snippets of news coverage. Emergency flashes. Breakthroughs. I wait for them to report my letters to the police, to the city leaders. I've told them about the army, about the murderer stalking the streets. I've given them all they need to find him.

Yet there is nothing. Every few days, another killing is announced. A new face to turn away from. Another of her copies torn apart as he rips his way through, tearing towards her.

I stand at the windows and try to see our apartment, perched up in the highest part of the city.

There is nothing to see. In the hospital, the outside world doesn't exist. The city isn't there. We are enclosed in steel, glass, fences and walls. Beyond there is just a blur of fog and neon.

There are various therapeutic methods they use to try to recover my memory. They think I am an amnesiac now. The sessions with the doctor continue. Each interrogation just a flurry of faces, a surging river of words.

I think of that flood as I float in the hospital swimming pool. Several other patients around me, all on their backs, eyes closed as soft thrumming music is played and a therapist talks in a murmur.

I repeat my name to myself.

I repeat her name to myself.

The two things I cannot let them take from me.

The sounds of those two words bleed into each other. They mix like my blood, until my low voice is sputtering the same garbled word—over and over.

The chemical blues and flickering shades, throwing light and shadow as I sink slowly under the surface. And my head going under the bath water. Held under an ice cold shower. Tasting the sharpness of that water pouring into my mouth, making my throat tighten. And all I see are rotten drains, and streams full of rusty old cars and dead dogs. Here a sprawling landscape of waste and decay, spilling out over the sides of a shallow pool. Dead grass and trees. Savaged, scorched fields as far as the flat horizon. A sky spitting black blood. Splintering. Splitting into shards of glass. A window shattering through to—

And the spectre of the doctor picking his way through the filth, waist-deep in the bubbling brown excrement. He pulls his way through. He claws at the red earth around him. It leaks dark blood over his hands. Weeps thick. And his mouth churning. Twisting. Chewing on something between those dull, blunted, yellow teeth.

An arc of amber light and I thrash in the water. A hand breaks the surface, smacks something. I go limp and sink.

Caught in plastic.

A calmness. The kind of hospital calm you're supposed to feel, but never really do. Always the anxiety. Always the noise, and the smell of something wrong. Drowning is quiet. It is solitude. Falling through light and through softness. Falling through blue and violet, through brilliant white. Like an echo, or a shiver on a crisp winter day. And so slow. A long drawn out kiss. My entire life has been a drowning.

She's watching me as I fall. Her smile so vibrant and red, warming me through the heavy curtains of cold that envelope me. A welcome. A beckoning. And I wonder if she too is drowning. Falling deep down into the dark of ocean at my side. Together we will sink into the soft sea bed and roll into the sediment.

Falling more.

Falling further through space.

Until at the heart of the universe—a chasm that devours everything brings us home, and crushes our bodies into the same matter.

Pristina liked to think of us as all the same dust. All the same ash. She would stare into the night sky and draw shapes with her hands, joining stars into new constellations. She said she felt as though she were bleeding dark matter, but she could never explain what she meant. As if her mouth were stretched wide as a thick black tar pushed out of her body, something that sucked life out of everything. She was terrified of giving birth to horror.

Instead an army of one. A multitude of her own self. Driven by rage, and committed to tearing the world apart. Not a horror, she would say — self-defence.

Yet a horror pursues her. A shadow that lingers and taunts me. Who then birthed that into the world?

Here I stop falling and pain sears through my lungs. Choking on acid. Vomiting into the pool. Scrabbling and clawing and snatching. Feeling hands grabbing at me. Holding my arms, and dragging me. Voices chanting in animalistic barks and howls. And I am heaved up. I am lifted and raised.

Into the air.

Into the light.

Such a soft shuddering of limbs.

Wrapped now and laid out. Not sure if I'm breathing. I open my eyes and the side of the pool is red with my blood, streaked in my vomit. My body shakes and pushes blue and violet light from my throat. My lungs burn as I breathe again. My blood is full of razors.

I return into the noise and rage of hospitals.

I could make a list of all the mistakes. I could write it out on the walls of my room—in all the rooms of the hospital, across all the smooth floors. I could etch them forever in the stone and plaster. Smear them in my own blood. Stark and red and forever. I could build a tower that climbed high into the heavens, so high it would challenge God Himself, and fill it with all my failures, all my lies.

Even that would collapse. Even that would fail. As I do, each and every day. With every breath. Each heart beat. A betrayal.

And yet I live with my mistakes. I am a scar—a wound that seeps the thick black shit of failure. With Pristina I learned how to use that for a powerful purpose, to direct it towards a goal. Her ability to channel that negative energy, to take an emptiness, a lack of, and create something from it. That is her gift. She took that from within herself and filled her life with purpose.

Maybe all I am is failure. All I can ever hope to be is failure.

And maybe that's my gift.

There are no mirrors in the hospital. I haven't
seen my face in—

There are no mirrors in our apartment. I never
see my face.

I have never seen my face.

I imagine my face is a thousand different
things—

The façade of a great pyramid.

The surface of the sea.

A flat overgrown lawn.

I imagine it is blank space. There used to
be eyes and a mouth and a nose—features,
recognisable. Now they are empty. They
are flat and smooth. When I put my hands
there, I can feel shapes, sense the void of my
mouth, hard teeth. But I only feel them with
my fingers. My body and mind do not register
their presence. Those forms are alien.

My face is the surface of a moon. A gas giant.
Formless and ever shifting. Even if there were
mirrors, I would see a swirling maelstrom of
red and purples, angry bruise colours in a one
hundred year storm.

And sometimes—I catch my image as I move passed windows, and there is a glimpse of something, a flash of light. A suggestion of a shape.

And sometimes—I stare into the water, the undulating surface of clear blue, and something looks back.

Sometimes that face is one I know is not my own. Sometimes I find myself staring into the black, empty eyes of the doctor.

Sometimes I am wearing the face of a horror.

I am brought to be interviewed by two men who claim to be from the police. Uniforms, and the same grinding language that makes the walls creak and my ears sing—the same language as the doctor.

They ask the same questions as the doctor. They show me the same photographs.

I shake my head until I am dizzy, until the room spins faster and faster. No— No, I say. I tell them they should already know everything. They have all the letters I sent them. They should be out there catching the murderer— my arm flies out wildly to point to where the city is, to where I think the city still is. I knock a cup half full of coffee with my hand. It crashes against the wall, splashing brown liquid. I watch it slowly pool on the floor.

They say they don't know about any letters, and they exchange expressions. Two blank police faces. Two bureaucratic blurs.

They sit and watch me as I tell them all about the murders, and the army of Pristina's copies, and the doctor that hunts them, seeking her.

I tell them about the wave of blood drowning the city.

They make many notes. As I talk for hours,

mouth so dry, arms moving, waving. Read my letters, where are my letters. My desperate pleas to them to do something. Make an arrest.

To protect her.

The doctor walks into the room and I fall silent. They stand together near the door. They talk and look at each other for long moments. When their eyes meet they fall silent. And the whole hospital falls silent. They look at me, all three, nodding, some thin smiles are shared, as well as the notes they made.

I am a failure. I am a body of failures. Mistakes built up over decades.
My life is a drowning.

The two police officers leave, and the doctor takes their place opposite me.

His face is my face.

His face is a television screen—static and interference and noise. His mouth opens and the screeching is that of a hundred tormented birds. Amber light burns up the wall behind him and he closes his mouth.

Now, he says, as he slides a photograph of Pristina across the table towards me. Tell me all about her.

I must remain silent. I will not be this mistake.
I will not become this.

Instead I leap out of my chair, throwing it
across the room as I roar abuse at him. The wall
is against my back, I'm trying to be as far away
as possible. Slow motion spittle in the wake of
my thunderous words. The clatter of metal on
stone as my chair crashes and shatters.

Brown coffee slowly running down the wall.

The doctor says nothing. He is an engine idling.

Then hands move swiftly across the table. The
photograph of Pristina is removed, and in its
place are placed several scraps of paper. One
after the other. Notes written in pencil.

I can't accept it at first. I refuse. They can't be
the same letters. He can't possibly have taken
them. Or else—

Taking a step forward, towards the desk.
Closer to the notes and closer to him. To his
face and that smell.

All the letters I had given to you. All the details
and information for the police. All given up to
him. And I can only be betrayed.

So I shrink back down to the floor. My rage is

spent. The fire inside me is dying out.

Sinking now to the sea bed alone.

A vast field. A flat expanse that stretches into the distance in every direction. The grey blurs on the horizon—a threatening vanishing point. The hospital fades into water—a clot of black blood dispersing into washed out ashen tones. Crimson light descends from a starless sky. The air—choking and murderous.

Something terrible happened here on this field. Some terrible crime was hidden and buried beneath the grass and bleeding red sky. And no one comes here anymore. It is a dead and empty place. A place lost to memory. To history. It lies beyond the limits of sight.

And rising from the earth of the field, the rank, heavy aroma of something rotting. Something buried deep below, decomposing and churning in the dirt. You can feel it in your bones, in your teeth. A rumbling. A deep shuddering that starts very low, in both frequency and in your body. Then it begins to slowly burn its way through you. Rising higher and higher in pitch. Until all you can do is kneel amongst the tall, grey grass and scream soundlessly at the raw sky.

And the images that speed through your mind, of concrete and white render, the cheap hospital looks of glee and sinister sexual appetites, destroyed faces photocopied and reprinted on medical reports, sitting at desks taking notes, legs crossed, a knowing nod and a bureaucratic smile, so slow it takes eons. The terminal music of a dying age. The city in ruins at your feet, ground down under centuries of decay, memories crushed into dust, the great gears of psychiatric machinery, scattered like the seed of a generation over this great lost field. No water to make it grow. No nutrition here. Just the scarred remains of an echo, a memory, a shadow blasted against stone.

If history is a highway, and we are the cars speeding along through the years, then this place is a jack-knifed lorry, skewed across all the lanes, spewing fuel. A twisted wreck of metal and misery.

I can see her there amongst the trees, a mere shape suggested by light shafts through broken branches. An arc of chemical blue, like medicine in water slowly dissolving, and she melts away into the gloom, a laugh carried on the air by startled birds.

Plunged into a bathtub of freezer water, hands flailing at the sides, desperately seeking a grip on the oddly slick side.

The taste of blood.

We bruise the air as we walk through the gardens. We blotch it all with sullen blue and black. It rolls over and burns through, purple and pointed. And when you speak it's like speaker shriek.

You stop walking and I keep going. I'm hearing you but I can't listen. I don't want to know the excuses or explanations.

Just the walled garden. Just the looming hospital building. Just me and the sky and the birdsong. The stillness.

I touch the wall, the red brick crumbles slightly against my fingertips. I feel you approach behind me. Your voice phasing, like whalesong.

I tell you that I wish I could dream.

You say nothing.

The wall is cold, and if it were ice then it would come as no surprise. A towering curtain of frozen silence, encircling the hospital complex. And outside, the city—living, breathing, pulsing with blood and tar. Within—we all shiver. We all ache.

You tell me it's probably the medication, that maybe speaking to the doctor would help. I need to open up.

Crawling up the wall, a thick black centipede. It darts between weeds growing between bricks. A flurry of legs and a shiny dark body. I watch it scurry higher, towards my hand, flat against the wall. You're talking, but the sound of those hundred legs scratching and clawing against stone. The mandibles working. It pauses by my thumb—a moment of hesitation. Then a shiver as it moves over my hand, the skin tickling, those hundred legs like tiny pins.

It continues on it's climb up the wall. I watch it get higher and higher, until it is gone, over the top and into the world beyond.

You have to help me get out of this place.

Why can't you blow apart these walls with your words?

Why can't you erode this concrete with the acidity of your touch?

Why can't your breath sear through all this steel and burn away all the wood and plaster walls?

I am an insect, crawling up a wall, desperate to escape but lacking the hundred legs I need. I am always falling. I have no grip.

You watch me. Silently, with the stillness of space. Each time I climb, each time I fall. This body is made of failures. A hundred. A thousand. So many broken and fractured moments. And you motionless. You statue. You form of bronze and steel. Taller than I can see, rising towards the sun.

And so I slip, and I fall again and again. And I break. Some day I will shatter into a hundred pieces, each one a furry black spider that will run for the cracks in the earth. And as eyes, I will stare out of the dark.

Why can't I summon the rage to tear down these walls?

Why can't I channel venom and spit and fire,

to engulf this all in flame?

Why can't I breathe free of walls?

I'm lying here. I lie. My room is blue and white and too much daylight. Falling through bedding. Falling through sheets and blankets. Bound by medication. Bound by restraints.

I am always falling.

That lurch in the stomach. The sensation of speed, the popping in the ears, blood rushing. Nothing rushing towards me but the unknown. The dark future.

All this time travel is too much. The human body isn't designed for it. We were never intended to move like this. We are meant to be static, stable, reliable. Solid. I am precarious, out of balance. It was what Pristina saw in me. It was what we shared. She was so like me. Or I was like her. Now all this shuddering and shattering, breaking me apart. I am huddled and hiding.

Now the falling stops. A soft landing. An embrace. And covers are pulled back, as light flashes and blinds. I don't struggle against the hands, the gentle touch that reaches me, fills me with a warmth. When I open my eyes, your face breaks the surface of the water, and I see you for the first time.

You are her. You have always been her.

I have fallen and you have caught me. You have found me, at last. And you hold me so close, and I feel your skin. Your hair.

You and yet not you. A copy.

She has been moving through all of them, all her copies, searching. The hundreds and thousands of scattered duplicated souls, this city full of her. And now finally she has found the one closest to me. Here. Where the doctor lurks.

You tell me you know the danger, and I leap from the bed in panic, raving—he will find you. Find her.

And already searching, the unblinking surgery eyes of that sleepless hunter. Red-rimmed and bleary. Bloodshot and yellowing. A movement of amber light in the depths of the hospital.

He stirs. That dragon now crawling through corridors. A great fire is beginning to rage.

You drag me back to the bed, your eyes flaring and intense. I can see Pristina inside. I can see her screaming through, lying in a bed of red-black, twisting bedsheets into knots in her hands, legs curling, whole body arching.

You tell me there is not much time. That you

can get me out but the body, the copy, will die. I must do as you say without question.

I touch your face. And the coiling of Pristina's body, her snaking in her bed of blood and tears. Across the city I can hear her screaming. I can feel the vibration of it. And the walls begin to crack. The window glass starts to sing a shrill song.

Your eyes are becoming deep and dark and dead looking. Your mouth is opening in slow motion. The roar of the doctor tearing through the corridors drawing nearer.

You take my hands in yours, and the shuddering is moving through you as well. Everything now is oscillating at an incredible frequency, beginning to shake apart. Dust and fragments of plaster fall away from the ceiling and walls. The windows are cracking. Your grip tightens and your eyes become completely black. And from your mouth comes a low moan, as your body starts to spasm and convulse.

Pristina's scream will shatter the world. This I have known since the beginning of her war. And now she screams through her copy, through you, smashing this room, this space, this air. The price is your body. And as I watch, blasted by the power of the sound she throws through you, you start to collapse. You start to disintegrate and fold.

Two screams now. Pristina and you. Phasing in and out of sync. A horrific cacophony stripping the room apart.

And you become a single point, a compressed moment in time and space.

And you fall silent.

But the room still peels away, falling into what was you. And far away Pristina's wail is a call, a song, urging me to go.

To escape through you.

And so I let myself be lifted, to be pulled towards your gravity well. And I fall into you. Fall through you. And behind, the room becomes a destroyed scene, a splintered mess of bureaucracy and medicine, blackened and charred by the rage of the doctor, bursting now through walls and doorways. Much too late.

So you collapse completely. You seal. And I know that in that room now there is a scene of butchery.

Pristina knows this too. She will release herself from the connection to you, a weeping, bloody rage filling her. The whole apartment will

shake at her anger. And the city will feel her
burning vengeance.

Falling—

As though through space.

Through the ocean.

Through time.

Falling—

Into something deep and bottomless. Swallowed. This mouth and throat. Towards a stomach.

This body a drowning.

This body in flight.

Sacrifices are made, and are necessary, during war. That's what Pristina told me once. She didn't like losing copies—replicas they may be, but still people, still living and breathing and suffering. She must have had no alternative in the hospital. She will have known he was close, that he would find the copy, destroy it. Murder her again.

Another face photocopied in black blood. Another headline.

And I know I cannot return to her now. Free of that place, I am, but I would lead him straight to her. So I must fall, perhaps forever. Out of time and space. Shifted. Out of phase. I will feel her resonate, but she will be intangible to me. And maybe I can lure him away, be a distraction.

She will raze everything to ash.

Millennia in free fall. In dreamless sleep. A black horizon never to be reached.

Then a beating. A throbbing. The heart inside waking, pulsing. Light beginning to blink. Across the horizon, becoming a twinkling. A flashing.

And I blink my eyes. Wipe away the ash and filth of centuries. The burial dust.

A sparkling distance now racing towards me. A city taking shape. Forms of buildings and towers and streets emerging from flat black. And sound and vibration. And breathing. My breathing. My lungs heaving.

Brilliant blue and neon, streaking through me. Falling now towards a moment.

I blink.

And I brace myself for the where and the when, as the world becomes solid, becomes real, blurs into shape around me.

I blink.

Now I hide in this secret place, in a city above the city. These halls, rooms, empty offices, warehouses—all long abandoned and forgotten, left to rot and gather dust. Amongst the waste, moving from place to place, avoiding the ever searching eyes, the clawing vision of the doctor. He hunts all these long days. He hunts for me, to lead him to her. He has the iron itch of my blood in the back of his throat. It has sunk deep into his translucent white meat. I hear his agonised roars late at night, as he thrashes through the city below. I crawl into dark places and cover myself in dirt and rubbish. I cover myself in the dark shadows of empty buildings.

I have seen inside him. I have seen through that shell and into the mind. He is a soulless creature. Nothing exists inside him, just a vast emptiness, a flat field of black grass. He is a barren, irradiated landscape. When he touches you he leaves toxic burns, and your skin strips away. Poisonous saliva oozes from that rent of a lipless mouth. At night he moves slow like an insect, his brain buzzing with millions of terrible wings. He is my dream every night. I can't escape his image. Under sweat-stained blankets, filthy and rank, my body flashes and twists, his face sawing jagged cuts through my mind. The echo of her name repeating.

And I wake with a cry caught in my throat,

early morning light bleeding through the smeared dirt windows of these high lost floors. I see her for a few brief moments, caught in the gate of the window frame. And then she too fades from view. She too dissolves into the weak yellow.

I wonder if she yearns for me the way she used to. She used to lie with her head on my breast, listening to my breath, to the pounding of my life. Her dark hair would spill over my body, spreading and pooling over me. In the nothing light of the city it became blood.

But all these days now. The only presence I feel in this city is him.

I never stay long in any one place. A day or two here—move to another. These are the long forgotten rooms above the city, the floors and staircases blocked off and bricked up, storage spaces left to ruin. When you walk through the city below and look up, you can see the grimy windows and boarded up floors, overgrown with weeds, home to flocks of birds. Below me, the occupied floors buzz with music, coffee shop chatter, the life of people moving. Below me there is light, crisp and sharp. I press my face to the ageing plaster partitions between hidden staircases and shop floors, listening to the sound of people. Warm air and cold shafts of light break through the gaps, the obscure suggestions of movement. I sit there for long moments, eyes closed, trying to remember what it was like to be real.

I move through these hallways of dust alone, a ghost, the only man alive in his very own city of ruin. I see the marks of others, footprints in the dirt, smears of hand shapes across walls and in the broken bathrooms. I never hear them. If they are here, they hide well. Better than me. Sometimes I wonder if I am seeing my own footprints—endlessly following myself around this warren in the sky.

All these places interconnect. This city is as joined up as the one it sits above. The streets here are corridors between buildings, passages from attic spaces, walkways across rooftops. When I emerge into the night air, above the glowing reds and blues of shopping malls, the fresh air makes me dizzy. I cough for long minutes, spitting black. My lungs feel heavy and full of the erosion of years, of decomposing office waste. I wipe a slick smudge across my mouth, feeling vulnerable in the open, even though high up. My scent will travel on the air, the doctor will catch it, nostrils will flare. Below, in the city of dust, my aroma is obscured.

I descend into the next stairwell, down into another shadow building, back to safety. Into darkness. Into the grime of a nothing existence. Locked doors give way to pressure, to force. I break through plaster walls and partitions. I find new rooms in dirty yellow, new windows that offer views across jutting buildings and curving architecture. The cityscape—a soft sensual silhouette in the amber of early evening.

There are amazing places hidden here. Places long shut away and faded from memory. Beautiful places. Above the tacky lights and garish plastic of a discount clothing shop, there is the memory of a theatre, a memory carved in plaster and stone, laced with cobwebs. The once plush seating, mould-eaten and wasted provides a comfortable shelter for several nights, and I lie here before the stage, imagining the performances that took place many long years before. For the first time in many weeks, I smile. I allow myself to relax for a time.

In this dark cavernous space, dancers and singers move through columns of light, pirouetting across the now rotten wooden floor. Shadows are cast around me. The warmth of stage lights fills me. High above, gossamer-whispered chandeliers sway gently to the sound of an orchestra, a spiritual music drifting through decades, reverberating around the theatre, billowing curtains of heavy purple velvet. And when the show is over, there is a wave of applause from the seating—a crashing, a hissing.

I stop clapping when my hands start to hurt.

Up here in this new space, there are desks and cubicle partitions. The mess of an abandoned office space swept into corners, old phones and fax machines. The black dust of toner colours the dirt on the floor. The air smells sweet—a memory of new carpets. As I walk through the ruin, other marks appear. Here there are burns, scorches, the stain of smouldering flames. Here are broken desks, shattered by great force, snapped by great rage. I see now the smashed windows, the scattered fragments of exploded ceiling lights. The massive corpse of an air conditioning unit lies broken and twisted, a mangled metal lump, the orange-red staining of rust growing.

Something happened in this place. The air here is heavy with absorbed fury. Like static, it feels charged. My skin prickles, mouth dries out. Somewhere very far away a high pitched whining, a siren wailing.

Hovering in the doorway to the office is a large black dog. I think of the doctor, of his salivating mouth that twists and churns. Of locked knees and the thrashing of nightmares.

Now the dog growling, glaring. Its movement from the doorway slow, threatening a pounce. I back out the way I came, my feet clumsy, not breathing, not looking away from that mass of clotted black, bristling hair.

And I run. Back through the ruin of the office, back up the staircase, back onto the roof, slamming shut the door behind me, leaning back against it in breathless alarm. Slowly now, feeling the anxiety of being outside creep back. So exposed. The orange glare of city, the swelling of grey across the sky. Such a bruising arc, lashed each day by the sun.

The doctor must be on my trail, the wreckage

of the office below left in his wake as he hunts through the city. All the more reason to not spend long in the open, not now, not here. The vast firmament, coiling above, feels so much like a huge eye staring down, never blinking, never resting.

The old theatre is the safest place I know. Only there have I ever felt at ease, never feeling the ominous presence of the doctor's search. So through the city I move, fast and as quiet as I can. Through the halls and warehouses of waste, across the rooftops, skirting chimney stacks and air conditioning units, humming loudly. Convinced the dog is on my trail, convinced it is him, I am always looking over my shoulder, always pausing at every noise to check. Sometimes I just run blindly through doorways and into rooms of dust, driven by fear. I trip and tumble through ruin and collapsed walls, the plaster and brick grit sucked down into my chest. I cough and choke, pushing on, night growing darker and the glow of the city blossoming into a white aura.

I have watched the people of this city move around below me. I have seen them move as grey blurs shifting through streets on rain-washed mornings. I have sat in the broken, filthy windows of ruined places and watched them working at desks, at computers, at meetings, at all kinds of machines. In office buildings high and polished, they drink coffee and they massage weary brows. I scan those faces as closely as I can from my perches around the city, some part of me hoping that I will catch sight of Pristina. I wonder how many of the faces I stare at each day are her copies. How many of them are part of her army.

When I close my eyes I see her floating on water tainted blue by chemicals and medicines, traces of indigo glimmering like the movements of fish too fast for the eye. She moves her hands through the cold water, her skin pale, fingernails cracked and broken. She smiles at me, and her eyes brighten with a vibrant blue that seeps into her through the water, burning in her irises. Under warm neon lighting I trace a route over soft curves, a slick pathway of shimmering wet that tastes of fresh photocopy and sweat. She moves slowly beneath my body, like a stretch, like a yawn, but I know is a sigh — long and drawn out. She is tinted in orange, but I know she is white and bruise-coloured blue.

I open my eyes. Moments like these are frozen—captured in concrete. Abrasive, they tear at your memory, leaving wounds that bleed continuously, like a paper cut in the brain. And time leaks out in a dribble, a slow puncture in personal history, deflating the whole of your life, until you are left—

—a dry shell—

—a bureaucrat—

—a nameless surgeon—

—a desk clerk—

— photocopying documents all day.

I have thought of stopping her. Of trying. I wander rooftops under the glare of the open sky, muttering over imagined conversations. To plead with her. To beg her. Stop this. End all the war, all the anger. There's so much of it in the world. And I hear her replies ricocheting from the stone buildings. How I am too weak. Too pathetic. How I am worthless to stand by her side in this fight. How much I am a failure in her eyes.

And so I wonder, for all this to end, would Pristina have to end?

The curve of the theatre holds me safely within its walls. I curl amongst the soft seating, breathing alone in the darkness. Shafts of light break through the high ceiling, here and there picking out sections of wall, plasterwork, worn wooden flooring.

Here there is silence. The city below seems not to really exist. So I can close my eyes and allow sleep to overwhelm me. I allow myself to relax.

When I open my eyes I instinctively know time has passed. The colour of the light is different. The angle it breaks through, shifted. I have slept, but I have no idea for how long. Hours, or days, it could be either. It has been so long since I experienced a sleep without dream or without the numbness of medication.

There is an aura about this place. Almost as if it were cut off from the rest of the city—above and below. It exists in its own space and time. And within I can take refuge. Find some peace from all the external turmoil.

And so this now will be my home.

This feels like a dangerous thing to decide. Remaining in one place for too long as has always come with risks. But I think this place is different. Even sitting here, surrounded by the cobwebs and curtains of plush purple, I

get no sense of the doctor's scraping, blasting
eyes. I don't feel his claws picking towards me.
There is just nothing.

I fill my new home with the things I've found scattered across this abandoned city. With blankets and bedding, lamps, space heaters, notebooks, and worn, tattered novels found in the forgotten storage space above a bookshop. The lamps and heaters fill the theatre with soft yellows and warming reds.

My days are spent scouring the empty places for supplies, stealing food from the city below, and looking for signs. Of the doctor. Of the copies. Of Pristina.

I find an old map of the city in a warehouse attic space, and spread it out on the floor of the theatre stage. I pin it in place, and mark out my locations across the city. The places I've been, the danger zones, vantage points, places to steal food.

And signs. I plot out sightings and glimpses of the doctor and his agents.

The doctor leaves many marks and symbols that betray his presence—

Scorch marks on walls.

The sounds of machinery roaring across the city at night.

Occult symbols in blood or tar, smeared on walls or windows.

The smell of ozone.

Dead animals in drains, alleys, and attics. The corpse of a small bird, nailed to a wall in an empty room high above the city, windows on all sides looking down on the below.

Hand prints in the dust covering the floor of a cavernous warehouse, as if someone had walked the entire space on their hands, never once righting themselves. I followed those prints as far as I could, until they led me to a broken wall and a fall into blackness. A rotten stench. A feeling of dread.

The amber streetlights. Glinting and flickering, like gas lamps, smearing the cityscape with greasy, pornographic light.

The howl of a dog. For hours. Me sitting on the rooftop listening. Shivering in the cold night.

The bodies. The many bodies piling up all over the city. Pristina's copy army slowly, methodically slaughtered. Each scene is marked on my map. I track the cases through old newspapers left around the city, from the bits and pieces of radio or television news I catch through gaps in walls.

I must try to put a stop to this. These murders must stop. Sooner or later he will get to her. One of the copies will give her away. I must find a way to break the secret of his crimes.

The tourist map is too small for the amount of information I am gathering and tracking. So I am marking the city out across the floor of the theatre stage. With thick black tape and paint, sketches of locations, salvaged photographs of the real places from newspapers and books. For some locations I have built small dioramas from model kits and plastic waste.

I can walk this map myself. I can move about it on the stage, picking barefoot from this rooftop to that, descend to an alleyway, observe a murder scene.

Within this map I can feel him, but the relationship is reversed. Now he is the hunted. And I stalk him around his hiding places, sensing his unease, knowing he is beginning to understand.

I have found that certain lights keep him from entering some areas. So I use what lamps I can and angle the light through coloured paper, or paint their shades and bulbs. It's the blue lights that keep him at bay. From light blues to violet, I wash the map in these tones, chasing him out of my main routes, my favourite locations to watch the city and its people.

But I only have so many lamps. And the location of Pristina's apartment—our apartment— glares at me from the stage. I have deliberately left this area blank. Just an emptiness. As if acknowledging its existence would draw attention to it. And I have no way to reach it from this abandoned city above. It lies outside the heart of the city, in the twilight zone of tenements and apartment blocks. I wonder sometimes if it really occupies our universe. Its impossible geometry. That cavernous interior. I think maybe it exists in a pocket of some other dimension, one willed into existence by Pristina. When we needed somewhere safe to escape to, she found it. Only now it is threatened by the doctor and his space-time shifting.

Maybe I can find more lighting and corner him, keep him trapped.

Maybe I can imprison him within a boundary of brilliant blue.

Sometimes my nights in the theatre are awake and busy. They are planning and arranging the map. I move lights and redirect colour, attempting to keep the doctor out of parts of the city. Experimenting with controlling his movements. If I can do this, then I may be able to protect Pristina's copies. If only I knew where they were.

Sometimes my nights are sleep. They are dreamless and quiet. I hunker down amongst my bedding in the rows of seating, wrapped in blankets and bathed in warm umbral light.

Now sometimes my nights are fractured with sound. With movement. I wake in a stutter. Panic rising in my throat as a column of smoke from a raging inferno. Grasping at seating, with flaring eyes in the blue light of the theatre.

And I see nothing.

I see the oceanic colour washing through the space. The drifting dust.

These nights increase in regularity. I begin to wonder the sense of remaining here. Perhaps I was wrong to imagine this place safe. The doctor must have found a way through the blue barriers. Found a way to get through to me.

Now it is every night. It is night after night of silence broken by the sound of grinding gears, of limbs caught in machinery. And the flashing of white light. Sudden strobing across the space, followed by the reek of ozone.

And I feel shifted. Subtly out of phase. Drunk. Shaking my head only makes it worse, and I fall into the theatre aisles, gasping, exhausted.

And I press myself against the wall, but the wall feels indistinct, like it isn't really there. I watch as around me the theatre fades, shifts, ghosts. Space is thinning around me. Time is breaking down, and I can reach through and see between moments. I can see between the ages.

It lasts seconds but seems like hours. I see the theatre packed with people. They move around me, through me. They are phantoms with light pouring through their bodies. A play takes place on the stage, the actors moving through my map. All my lamps and models, untouched by their performance. A silent applause erupts, and I find myself joining them. I find myself in tears.

When it ends I'm slumped. I'm drained. I crawl back to my bedding and bury myself.

I hope it happens again.

I hope it never happens again.

This thinning is happening everywhere now. Not just the theatre, but all across the city of the above.

On rooftops I witness vistas of a city of the past, all industrial chimney stacks and smog.

In warehouses and attics, I hide amongst ghostly crates and boxes while the apparitions of workers move stock around, smoke cigarettes.

In abandoned offices I am part of a group of employees taking part in meetings, sitting at desks entering data into computers, photocopying documents.

From my vantage points I watch the city of the below for signs it is happening there too. How can the people not see or feel these changes, these shifts? Are they so dulled and numb? So blind?

The city appears still. Oddly quiet. Nothing suggests the thinning is there or spreading or that it is noticed. Over days I scour newspapers. I descend from an attic space into the backroom of a café, where I manage to steal a radio.

Now I can hear the coverage of the city. The

voices metallic and interrupted by static.
They don't mention the thinning space, and
the newspapers are concerned only with the
ongoing murders.

Reality is breaking down. Time and space are being fragmented and ground down. The walls of the universe are being stripped back, torn apart by raging claws.

Pristina lies at the heart of this tornado. A swirling mass of destruction—ash, tar, shattered concrete, twisted steel, seared flesh and bone.

A flap of wings and it is gone.

A blink and we phase back.

We glitch in and out of moments. Time is a flow, a river and we are swimming against the current. Overwhelmed now, our mouths are flooded with brackish water. And we cough, choke. When we vomit we can see through time.

She seeps black ink into the circuits of space-time-machines. Catching fire and melting. Disintegrating. We zoom out and see the city coil in flame. We see pavements become orange and buckle with streams of magma, boiling up through cracks.

The radios fall silent. There is just static. Just a haunting hissing. Sometimes a single voice deep in the noise calling out words that can barely be heard. Shouting out across the void of collapse.

A smashed television screen, sparking, wild blue and electric fire.

An office building engulfed in flames. Windows shatter with the heat. The steel framework buckles. It collapses into itself.

A room full of grey men in suits screaming. Blank, featureless faces. Their single wail oscillates at the same frequency of a black hole.

A news report on a series of acts of economic terrorism, repeating over and over and over, each repetition slightly more distorted than the last, the image twisting into noise and fuzz and black light that pours out of the screen.

Each day it gets worse. Pristina must be burning with so much fury now. She must be a star spinning so fast and violent. If I were to climb onto the rooftops and look towards her apartment, the arcing of neon and spinning red light would surely dazzle and blind me.

This is what she wanted. This is what I helped her achieve. I sit in this attic and watch as the shapes of people and objects ghost in and out of my vision, remembering how I invented the videotape method. Now it is just like the world is being recorded over, again and again. Times, moments, spaces—all occupying the same slice, the same spot on a loop. How much longer before it wears out and snaps, sending reality coiling and burning into infinity?

I wonder if she can really keep this up for long. If she truly has that much anger within her. Perhaps this will just fade out—a fire slowly smouldering to embers.

How much responsibility should I take for this? I didn't stop her when I could have. I didn't say no. I actively took part, encouraged her—so I could be close to her. To recover that unity we had before all this began.

A unity based on shared alienation. A sense we didn't belong.

I've always been a non-committal person. Never taking a strong position. You just want a quiet life, she'd say to me. And shake her head. Playfully, with a smile and a laugh. But I knew, even then, that beneath there was disapproval. Pristina always glowed with a passion for something. For ideas, books, films—for me. I was happy to simply bask in that glow.

This body a drowning.

This body of failure.

The world is thin.

So the seams appear. The joins between moments.

A little light leaks through—brilliant and white and pure. Surgery light. It peels along the length of the split, opening it up wider.

Hands covering eyes. Searing light but no heat. A cold light.

And you can step into the cracks. You can step through and into another moment.

This body in time travel.

Slipping through.

Along the flow of reality, a fantastic rushing of time, space, sound, light.

I stand before these walls and press my hand to the surface. The plaster is no longer there. My hand pushes through and I step into a void. The space shifts and I feel my gut lurch. My ears pop with a pressure change, and a new place opens up around me. It unfolds from a single point.

I am somewhere else.

I am sometime else.

I look behind me and see the theatre falling away. The city falling away. My life falling away.

This body in flight.

The skein of the universe is twisted. It's knotted and coiled. A myriad realities sit alongside each other. And as the fabric that separates them thins, it becomes possible to move through.

I can travel in time. I can walk through dimensions.

I have seen this city from many angles at once. I have walked its past. Through the fields that were here before there were people. Here I have stood amongst trees and flat plains of black grass, while in the sky a red sun glows and runs like a weeping sore.

I have stood and watched the city grow, from fishing village to industrial centre to financial and commercial hub. Wood giving way to stone giving way to glass.

Sometimes I watch this all in slow time. I see the years pass sluggishly. Sometimes I allow time to run so quickly that it all smears together, one blur of motion and time and space. I stop at random points to see what has changed. A new building here or there. A network of streets. The development of electric lighting.

It all runs softly through my fingers. I work these moments with my hands—pick out this image, that time, some other story that catches my attention. I caress and roll those flat moments to life. Bring them energy and vibrancy. I shudder with such energy. Teeth clatter—the sound of trams from the old days. And the long, slow hiss of steam from down by the river, the factories and shipyards, as my mouth opens and I shimmer. Just lights. Just sparkling neon swirling in a glass cylinder of black ink.

To shift through space now. To glide like the old sorcerers did. I can fold this city and move without moving. From the theatre base, to my observation posts on various building rooftops. To my old apartment.

And I hunt him down. I seek him out in these dark city hallways. Between the towering monoliths of commerce, backwards through the years. He can hide in any moment and in any time. He's always been this furious rent in reality, able to fold himself into the past. Now I can follow. Now I can do as he does.

Through folds in doorways and old plaster walls, wrecking through time, tearing into space and the past. He flees because he can sense something has changed, something more than the power I have to follow. He can sense that the strings holding everything together are becoming worn through, the membranes are thinning, beginning to rip. He knows what she is doing.

At last I can fight. At last I can join the struggle with her. Not by her side, as once before, but out here, in the field. I can harass and battle. I can pursue and be pursued. I can keep him away from her.

I see him twist through an alleyway and go after. The humming. The violet arcing light. The surging sound.

And he moves through a crowd on a busy cobbled street, his tailored suit standing out amongst the clothes of the old world. They don't see him. He is a ghost as am I. Together we will haunt this place until we leave. They will tell tales of us. Stories and books will be written.

He catches sight of me, and jump-cuts—a film breaking mid-scene. When I catch up, it is a field, a riverbank, and he is running through black grass as high as his chest.

I watch him from the top of a high tree. He spins and tumbles through the field, a parody of a child, mocking laughter over still air. He knows what I am doing. He knows and so he plays. He runs and dances and twirls. Taunts me.

We chase for hours. For days. Sometimes I am following him, sometimes he comes after me, a flaring, streak of amber light.

He stands on rooftops and towers. In howling gales and the pouring rain of this city's past, he laughs and dares me to follow once again. Always once more.

We play this game, you and I, he shouts across the sky. And lightning splits the heavens open, a silent arc followed by the terrible din of thunder that seems to come from his open, laughing mouth.

We fall. Over the edge of a building, through the air, tumbling over and over. I watch him far below me, cackling as he vanishes through air, a bruised wake of sky.

And I land hard in the back street of the city's now. The here. My own present.

The doctor steps over me, his laughter low and threatening. He drags another with him. This other man struggles, tries to cry out, but a gloved hand is securely over his mouth.

Both men stare down into the filthy alley, at the blackened shape that lies there—at me. One man's eyes are alive with fear. The other man, if it could even be called a man, has the wild eyes of the murderer.

I watch as he slits the man's throat, and throws his body to the ground—discarding trash.

And I see in those eyes. As the red pumps out of his neck across the ground, the walls—over me. As he lies there in the shit and blood. I see Pristina in his dying eyes. I see her lying in her bed, her face a dark wailing rent. And her scream tears through the brick of the buildings that rise around us. As another of her copies is butchered in front of my eyes, she shatters this street with a pulse of sound beyond human hearing.

Somewhere in space a black hole responds in kind.

The doctor has gone. In a moment of gurgling, of laughter, of pleasure. He folds himself and—

I blink.

It is as if the foot of a giant had descended from the sky. Perfectly flat. This street, once warehouses and empty tenements, now crumbled red brick and broken concrete. Smashed. Reduced. Nothing remains standing in a perfect circle. And as dust settles, I notice my ears ringing.

I look into the eyes of the dead man, and they are blank.

I look at my hands, and they are streaked red with my blood, his blood.

The faces of all the dead are burned black and red into my mind. As Pristina ghosted through them and saw them end, so I too saw her end within them. And a small part of her died along with each.

All their pictures hang from the walls of the theatre, poorly printed features in the black ink of newspaper headlines. Those flat eyes stare straight ahead, an audience of phantoms for the actors and singers on the stage. Sometimes I stand there and imagine myself some kind of performer. As if this were all just some elaborate play. As if this were all just fiction.

I move from picture to picture, repeating their names over, saying it out loud so all can hear—the stage, the audience, the map, the doctor, Pristina, the dead. So they know their own name. Too soon the dead are forgotten. Too soon their names slide into history, and they become just photographs. Footnotes. I say these names so I remember. And through them, through their shapes, I can reach her. Perhaps some part of her still connects to these lost souls.

Each night I repeat this. The walk through the theatre aisles. The sounding of the names. The calling. I put my hand to their faces. I touch the words of their names. The ink stains my skin. Sinks into my blood.

I am blood and ink. I am running thick with red and black. Just like she does.

I am a coiling. I am a spitting and burning. Arcing through time.

Then the days come when I pin up a new picture. Usually torn from the newspapers, heard on the news, or television, between coffee shop mutterings and banter.

This one though. This one is from me.

This one is just smeared red blood on dirty paper from the flattened alley. This one is in the blood of the dead, the murdered. No photograph. No newspaper clipping. Just this nightmare swirl.

I stand quivering in the blue light. The theatre audience are hushed.

I speak the name aloud. I rage it at the wall. Shout it so hard my throat aches. The plaster shudders and cracks.

This is the last. This is the end. I tell them all—every face, every audience, every performer.

I slump into my bedding, shivering, shaking, covered in the blood of a murdered man, churning with bees, a machine rattling. And as the plaster continues cracking, something inside me begins to rise. A heat. A buzzing. Up from the pit of my stomach. Through my veins—a fire. And my ears fume with the noise—a crashing waterfall, a collapsing tower, an exploding star.

And my mouth opens and black light streams towards the cracking wall. And the screaming in my head—it isn't me. It's her.
Pristina. Screaming through me.

Black light spills out. Cracks open up all across the city and it pours out over streets, runs down the walls, staining everything it touches like ink. And as it settles into pools it thickens into a tar.

At first they went unnoticed. Cities are full of broken roads and walls and buildings collapsing. Then stories circulated about sinkholes in gardens. In the middle of streets, opening up into deep voids and swallowing entire vehicles. People.

Dramatic, but people got over it. They moved on. As with all things. As with wars and political corruption and scandal. A moment of outrage. A petition. A march. Something to defuse dissent. Then it's gone.

Then, as a spider delicately and deliberately picks its way over skin, so small fractures began to sliver through the fabric of the city. Through thin plaster walls in apartments. Through the white render slabs on the flanks of the bureaucracy. Roads. Hospital car parks. Theatres.

And as Pristina's scream sears through me, directing all the boiling black bile at the broken wall, it burns through and surges through every crack and fracture across the entire city. Everywhere, black hole light is erupting.

I watch it all from the highest point of the city, a great radio tower climbing towards the curve of sky. Below, all the flashing, as neon, amber, white, red light is swallowed by blackness. A blackness that shines, somehow brighter than anything else. As bright and clear and pure as a night sky, starless and impenetrable. An eternity.

And it churns. It boils. The city streets consumed by it. The cloying sludge that bubbles up and steams. Climbing up walls now, cracking through brick and concrete. There's a hissing that begins very low, in places here and there, and it rises up. It intensifies into a chainsaw buzz. As an acid that blackness eats through everything it touches. It consumes all before it with a hunger, a fizzing.

A great sea turning over a beach in a storm.

A tsunami rising over a fishing town.

So much wailing and panic. So much noise. Of traffic and people. Their fear and fighting. One leading inevitably to the other. I close my eyes and imagine myself asleep. I imagine myself at her side, in her arms. At peace. I imagine a world so unlike all of this.

I sense the doctor fleeing this maelstrom. He is shifting through time, attempting to outrun it.

But this darkness is leaking through history. It is erasing everything.

There is nowhere—no time—to run to.

A television flickers into life.

A radio blares static for several sharp seconds.

There is a moment of still.

When Pristina appears on the screen, she has the appearance of someone caught in a moment of transformation. Between states of being. Gone is the haunted expression of her youth. Gone is the timid stance of someone hiding.

Here is a woman fierce. Here is a woman becoming.

And her sympathy has evaporated. Her humanity has left her. She will tear you apart. She will sear your flesh and render you ash in a blast of irradiated flame.

Some men collapse into spasms as soon as they hear her voice. Some men deny they even hear anything, and yet their ears still stream with blood.

Her mouth moves around dying stars. She uses the language of geology, shifting landmasses, and ancient insects that crawl and fly. Her words are swarms of teeth.

She addresses the city. Reads an account of

the failures and crimes, the disgraces. All their shameful episodes. She is impassive. There is no forgiveness left. None possible. Not now. Centuries have been endured. Centuries of excuses. Of selective amnesia. She has been screaming her whole life. She has been screaming—

In her single steady voice, a thousand other voices rage and roar.

In her single fixed expression, a thousand other faces twist and shudder.

Pristina is a colony. No one person. She is the many. The multiple at once. And when you hear her voice there are so many other words emerging at the same time that don't appear to be coming from her mouth. Her voice is a stream, broadcasting in a myriad languages— human, animal, ancient. You can't understand it with your ears or brain. You feel it. Your body reacts despite yourself.

Some people fall to their knees and vomit. Others begin to pray. Or beg. She speaks a single word with a hundred voices, and they shatter like sculptures in ice.

Her shape shudders with the presence of so many others. Those copies she brought into existence, gathered around her, that became her—their forms shimmer all around. People stare and swear they saw ten, twenty, thirty other people. They saw hundreds. They saw thousands. Still they can't believe.

Not until they see the city consumed by creeping black tar. Until they see their world devoured by the dark.

And I wonder. I see her on the television screen. I hear the voice on the radio. A blur of colour and a screech of white noise. I wonder where Pristina is amongst all this rage. I wonder if she has lost herself completely, swamped by her hundreds, her thousands.

It was always hard to tell where Pristina ended and her copies began. Where the join was. I had thought that she would rise above the sound of that clamouring army, to become a general or figurehead. To coalesce and solidify.

Now I realise that she has shattered into that ocean. There is no longer any individual. No self.

And I wonder why that terrifies me.

She stands so still, motionless in the greyness of the field. A scarecrow figure with the gold of dawn dappling the dew on the blades of grass around her. She opens her arms, sending a shock wave across the field, a deep bass boom rippling outward, soft as a kiss that leaves you breathless. As her eyes close, a calmness comes over her—the white face blankness of the coma patient, eyes moving rapidly behind closed lids.

She stands there amongst the grass, her lips barely moving as she mutters in a low voice, almost indiscernible, an ancient language of rock and time. Her pale blue lips seep ink, dribbling down her chin in thin streams as her muttering grows into a babble, the ink frothing and bubbling, spurting from her lips in deranged spitting gestures. It sprays over the grass, all over the field, hissing with broken machine noises, fizzing into the soil, turning the grass deep blue, causing it to wilt and rot.

She lifts her hands slow, palms up, fingers stretched out and nails long like steel talons. The field begins to rumble and rupture, the earth breaking, fracturing, the dead grass turning to dust like ancient paper dried in the sun.

Then a wave of energy blasts out from her across the field, a sonic boom in its wake.

Everything turns to red. Red with fire. Red with blood. Red with the neon blaze of a dying star.

She tears a hole in the fabric of history and rends everything with her nails, poisonous gas bellowing from her mouth as she spits foul blue ink into the layers of reality, bleeding it all together, ripping everything into a great soup.

To destroy, defile, deconstruct. She leaves everything black ooze and sludge.

Here it comes—pouring down the walls of the theatre. With the crack and hiss of electricity. With the nothing smell of space.

All the lights flicker and go out. A darkness broken only by faint moonlight through high windows.

Down these walls and to the floor. Footsteps through dry leaves as it moves slowly across the the theatre, filling all the space, reaching the high stage.

And all the sound is swallowed. All the city noise—the panic and fear, the violence of people. Is there really any city left? This theatre could be the last place left. The last piece of the city. Of the earth. Floating in the universe. No stars. Just a single supermassive black hole. Thrumming. Throbbing. A shattering hymn pulsing throughout time. Phasing through reality. And so many mouths open, full of that song, burning with it. Raised up and spraying the world with black light.

Here it comes—rising up towards me, at the centre of my map, drawing circles in red around Pristina's apartment location.

Here it comes—returning to claim me.

VOID

A roadmap of failures. A body of scar tissue. Define yourself through pain and suffering. Build a sense of self—strong and resilient. Face your challenges head on. Overcome. Endure.

This is where things fall apart. This is where everything breaks down. It's the point where matter loses stability, pulled apart by intense gravitational forces. The spaces in between grow larger.

Everything is emptiness.

Everything is void.

So when we walk through walls, there is nothing there to block our path. We are shapes holding dark energy in place. Merely skins. Beneath the surface—we vanish into the abyss.

If you enter me, I consume you. And you consume me.

Great mouths into the nothing.
Here we fall into the universe.

It's nearly over, she says. I consume you, and you consume me.

I watch from the high windows of the apartment. Below, the city is black. For hours I have stood and watched. For a while I wondered if I was expecting the city to return—lights to flicker back into life. But that won't happen. And I don't want that to happen. Soon the apartment will be gone too. And so will I.

I blink.

I don't know why we came here. My eyes opened and the sky was black, and when I sat up and saw the ocean rolling towards me, I saw that it was black too.

Like ink.

Like tar.

Pristina stands on the slate grey sand, a deep red shawl pulled in around her shivering body. She stares out across the sea. She is waiting for something.

I walk up and down the beach, keeping away from the dark waters rushing up towards me, constantly hissing and crashing and rolling back into the oceanic chasm. The sand is littered with hundreds of small black pebbles. They slip and slide in my hands, glassy and dark, yet something deep within them appears to smoke and coil.

I fill my pockets with the smooth stones. Gather them up in my arms and carry them back to her. I place them all carefully on the sand beside her, piling them up into a cairn. She watches with curiosity and sits down beside me, her hands on mine.

I ask her where we are, and she takes one of the black stones in her hand, turning it over and over.

She tells me that this is the edge. This is where everything falls away into the sea. Where everything is eventually ground down to sand.

She holds up the stone. This was the city, she tells me. Consumed in blackness, now broken down and tumbled through the seas. It will be worn and eroded down until it is the beach we sit on. Until it is the air we breathe.

And all the people? She pauses and smiles. Slowly she lifts a hand and points out to the churning waves.

Pristina is chasing pigeons around the roof of the shattered warehouse. She laughs as they flutter and flap away, shedding feathers into the darkness.

I watch this go on from a lawn chair, my sunglasses slipping down my nose. I tell her it's pointless, that they can see her coming when she tries to sneak up on them. She ignores me and giggles, creeping over the fragments of broken glass and concrete. She leaps at a couple of dirty looking birds, hands outstretched, and they squawk loudly and take to the air. Pristina stands looking disappointed.

This is the only building standing. Around us is just an empty field. A flat, blank, black space.

Pristina mixes another cocktail and lays out on her lawn chair, fixing her bikini as she stretches her legs and sighs. She puts on her sunglasses and take a sip from her tall glass.

Above us, the sky is torn apart by enormous glowing holes. Each ringed in angry red, pulsing, throbbing like a heartbeat. They bleed, seep, blur into one another, and we lie here basking in the crimson light.

A dead city washed with blood light.

Sometimes I wake up and feel myself melting away into pure energy. Into light. I hold my hands up before my eyes and they are transparent. They blur as I move them through space. I begin to ghost. And as those shapes twist before me, they sear in bright neon arcs, of violet and amber, and it blossoms like blood in water, until a blinding flare ignites and my body is engulfed in a cold burn of brilliant white light.

I lie naked on the cold grey sand. My face presses into the grit. Into that salted history ground down into dust. I breathe deep, and my lungs are filled with those lost years and faces. Through my body. Through my blood.

Pristina carefully, methodically, tattoos my body. Coiling black images move over my skin, from my ankles, up my legs, my back, travelling down my arms to my fingers. The black ink of the ocean. The black ink of time. For hours, I lie here, wincing, gasping as the needle pricks my skin over and over, and she gently dabs at me with a rag. Mopping up the excess. The red of my blood that runs, mixing with that dark ink.

I can't see what she is covering my body with, but I feel the twisting shapes slither through me. Snake and worm, smooth and slipping, great knots of looping bodies in a shimmering black. Some kind of strange symbols, in shapes I've never imagined, impossible angles causing my skin to collapse, my body to dissolve into light. A weird power moving through me, through tattoos so terrible. I stare at my hands, fingers digging into the sand, and the red of my blood pumps through those dark weaving lines. Eyes in my body glare.

I am many holes.

I am many mouths.

I am many eyes.

She tells me to turn over so she can cover the rest of me. I feel the sand sting my bleeding black as it is absorbed, churning together with the ink moving through my blood and skin.

I ask her what this is for. Her face moves over mine, blocking out the sky. This will protect you. This will let you fight him.

She tells me to close my eyes.

These glowing clouds of black fire. A column of smoke, choking and thick with grease and fat. The great reduction of human waste.

Here there is nothing but the fire, whipped by winds into a terrifying storm, churning around a central point. Just a star exploding over and over again.

And within this conflagration, the hospital sits. Empty. All patients gone. Or never there. Sometimes it's as though the doctor made them all up. How much did he truly lie about? Fictitious patients to support an out of control drug habit. To support his ego. His reason to exist. Now they are gone, and all the staff, burned up and consumed. All blown into the vacuum of space as cinders and ash. Glowing embers twisting for eternity through time.

And he writes and writes and writes. At his desk, huddled in corridors, curled on empty wards. He scrawls words in the blue ink of his blood, across walls and sheets and floors. He writes more lies into his patient files, with hands shuddering, with a brow sweating.

These words are all he has. They are all he is. When he bares his chest and roars at the white walls, the blue-blood shows through his thin pallid skin. And they are all lies.

He knows there is no one left to read them. No one here to listen to his untruth, to manipulate and fool. He has seen them leave, blacken and burst into flame. He has watched them walk free of him and his hospital walls. And he stood helpless, raging and cursing, a madness of filth and stained polyester shirts.

His own fiction has ended.

Though he cannot stop. To stop would be to cease to be. And he has always been.

This beach of grey sand. Now of glass. Now of mirror.

Now this bathroom, and a face reflected, distorted and bent.

A flash of colour in a monochrome world. We see things for a moment in a blur of motion. Something falls and there is a crash that slows into a roar of animals. Such barking resonating underground.

And the floor shudders.

And the floor turns red.

A neon light flickers, and I blink.

A bathroom. That hospital smell of chemicals and sickness. And a silence that blasts a hole through my chest, so deep and vast it feels.

Nothing lives here. Nothing stirs here. And it feels as though nothing ever really did. I touch the white of the sink, expecting it to fade away. But it is cold and hard. I look at the mirror and there is just a blur of black light.

My body of twisting black lines. These terrible tattoos moving, shadows beneath my skin. And I move naked through these hospital halls, a bristling static in my wake.

These corridors are dust and detritus, a wasteland of abandon. They were never alive. They were never more than a dream. Now they disintegrate into the lies they are. Collapsing. Breaking down. The floor is littered with the shattered glass of windows, the plaster and brick of the walls. Here papers and files, blue and red ink scrawled. I pause to read the words, but they make no sense. They are in a form unknown to this world. Black words in vulgar shapes. Any attempt to speak them out loud results in nothing but choking or hysteria. A bloody itch in the throat. Drinking drain cleaner.

I have come here to find him. To finally face him. To end him. Through me moves the thick ink of eternity. So powerful, endless, and yet empty.

I am a terrible nothing.

I am mouths and black holes.

Enter me and I consume you.

I enter you, and you are consumed.

And so it is. So this hospital now, breaking apart and drawn into me. A slow walk through the dark and flickering corridors, the plaster and brick stripping away and seared into ash, coiling through space into the abyssal tattoos bleeding across my body.

I am coiling black light.

A storm of raging black fire.

And I see them around me, the blurring, ghostly shapes of Pristina's others, her copies. They break free from my tattooed skin and tear this world down around me. Acid claws. Just great mouths that swallow. A maelstrom of surging, super heated air, melting reality before my eyes.

Corridors bend and distort. The window glass runs like thick soup. My fingers feel that hot plastic texture of the air.

The hospital folding into itself.

And the smell of fires burning through everything. The heart of the building just one great ball of flame, growing and spreading. Orange roaring through the passageways. Red licking at the white walls, scrawled in his blue words.

I think of Pristina, of her terrible screaming all through those nights in our apartment together. Of her song that tore the world to shreds.

My arms held before me, the swirling patterns of black and red sliding across my skin. Her song inside me. Her song injected into my skin, into the meat of my being. I am her hymn made flesh. Through me her voice shatters, reverberates, thunders with the power of a spinning star.

Here I am—a gravity well into which everything is sinking.

Outside the apartment there is nothing. I can see the nothing. Feel it. Nothing has a weight—it pulses gravitational energy. We are at the centre of a black hole. Our lights are blinking. We thrum.

Pristina is silent. Behind me somewhere in the labyrinth of rooms and corridors, she is waiting. Her nervous tension reaches me even here. The hair on the back of my neck bristles. The dark waves of ink on my body slowly twist into tight knots.

I press a hand to the window. It doesn't even feel cool any more. Nothing feels like anything any more.

I keep staring into the ocean of darkness. Hypnotic in its depth.

And as the lights in the room blink off and on again, a face in the glass flashes in and out of sight. Just a fracture of an image. A ghost.

It is not my face.

I remember dying—

In a car accident, alone on the highway, while arguing with my husband on the phone. I lost control and smashed into another car coming from the opposite direction.

Burned alive in my sleep.

In hospital, old and frail, of cancer, alone and frightened.

As an infant, of a birth defect, only a few hours old. Only long enough to see brilliant white hospital lights, and flashes of faces, uniforms.

Of an overdose, after a drunken argument with my boyfriend. I slit my wrists and sunk myself into a bath of cold water. The bloody red waves sloshed onto the white tiled floor.

Murdered, in an alley—by a man.

Lights flicker in the narrow corridor. Flashes of amber that strobe walls of yellow peeling wallpaper. In a small side office the doctor huddles in a corner, his shirt sleeves rolled up to the elbows. His skin is a sallow, Monday mourning white. Eyes ringed red, unblinking.

He breathes hard, sweating blue ink into his polyester shirt. He is watching the clock on the wall. It has stopped. He doesn't know how long he has been watching, waiting, for it to start moving again. The fear moves through his bowels. Locks in his knees. Time is his river, his flow. Now it is frozen and he is stuck. Powerless.

Caught in this moment. He's leaking ink from his nose and ears, haemorrhaging, staining his fingernails. His hands shake as he rubs a cold porn hand over his chin, smearing it across his mouth—a blue streak over lips like those of a corpse in water. He snorts and spits a thick glob of clotted bloody-blue onto the floor and looks back to the clock.
No movement.

His breath fractures the air with harsh rasping rakes, as the strobing amber lights in the corridor slow and finally blink out into darkness.

The doctor paints slow words in spastic hand

gestures, signals that form a cryptic geometry in the air, angles cut sharp as fractured window glass. But he is losing his words, losing his ghost talk. It slips away from him now, blinking out in pulses of burnt orange down the hospital corridor, a series of cigarette burns in the gloom. He is locked in one moment as his surgery-shit leaks from his veins, coughing into his hand. Blue-red smears on polyester shirt sleeves.

He is locked to this building, bound to the fabric of the hospital. Through time he drew his strength from its decay, from the years of psychological torment rendered down into paper and numbers. And now, as the hospital dies, he finds himself stranded in the final moment, in the wake of our flight, and he knows he has no road map to safety.

The building is shutting down—switching off. It's disconnecting itself from history. It will sing its song no more. The brick dust and peeling paint will drain from existence, their colour will disperse in the waters of space, until nothing remains of this place. Not even a memory. The field will reclaim the land, rolling over the dilapidated pile in a series of slow moving waves.

Pushing up from the bathroom floor, blood dripping from face, nose. A sound like rushing water. Vision blurred. Head aching.

Red water sloshing across the floor. Hands moving through, seeking support. Pushing up. Gripping the side of the bath to steady.

Water is pouring over the side.

And so I collapse into my self.

I am mouths.

I am holes.

I chew the universe over and over, and spit out a boiling mass of burning black tar. Something to sit and smoulder. Eventually cool.

A new star.

A new start.

And all that I was, everything I am, is used up and spent. I am burning away. The last thing left to fizzle out.

Enter me, and consume me, Pristina says.

About the Author

Kenny Mooney was born in Berlin when it was still divided by a stupid wall. He grew up in Scotland, England, and Cyprus. He is the author of the novella *The Gift Garden* and the novel *In the Vast and Boundless Deep*. He lives in York.

www.kennymooney.com